Snow White

Snow White

JENNI JAMES

Village Lane Publishing

PRAISE FOR JENNI JAMES

Beauty and the Beast (Faerie Tale Collection)

"Jenni James takes this well-loved faerie tale and gives it a paranormal twist. Very well written and hard to put down, even on my cruise vacation where I had plenty to do. Looking forward to others in Jenni's Faerie Tale series. A great escape!"
—*Amazon reviewer, 5-star review*

Pride & Popularity (The Jane Austen Diaries)

"This book was unputdownable. I highly recommend it to any fan of Jane Austen, young or old. Impatiently awaiting the rest of the series."
—*Jenny Ellis, Librarian and Jane Austen Society of North America*

"Having read several other young adult retellings of *Pride and Prejudice,* I must admit that *Pride and Popularity* by Jenni James is my top choice and receives my highest recommendation! In my opinion, it is the most plausible, accessible, and well-crafted YA version of *Pride and Prejudice* I have read! I can hardly wait to read the [next] installment in this series!"

—*Meredith, Austenesque Reviews*

"I started reading *Pride and Popularity* and couldn't put it down! I stayed up until 1:30 in the morning to finish. I've never been happier to lose sleep. I was still happy this morning. You can't help but be happy when reading this feel-good book. Thank you, Jenni, for the fun night!"

—*Clean Teen Fiction*

Northanger Alibi (The Jane Austen Diaries)

"*Twilight*-obsessed teens (and their moms) will relate to Claire's longing for the fantastical, but will be surprised

when they find the hero is even better than a vampire or werewolf. Hilarious, fun, and romantic!"
—*TwilightMOMS.com*

"Stephenie Meyer meets Jane Austen in this humorous, romantic tale of a girl on a mission to find her very own Edward Cullen. I didn't want it to end!"
—*Mandy Hubbard, author of Prada & Prejudice*

"We often speak of Jane Austen's satiric wit, her social commentary, her invention of the domestic novel. But Jenni James, in this delicious retelling of *Northanger Abbey*, casts new light on Austen's genius in portraying relationships and the foibles of human nature—in this case, the projection of our literary fantasies onto our daily experience."
—*M.M. Bennetts, author of May 1812*

Prince Tennyson

"After reading *Prince Tennyson*, your heart will be warmed, tears will be shed,

and loved ones will be more appreciated. Jenni James has written a story that will make you believe in miracles and tender mercies from above."
 —*Sheila Staley, Book Reviewer & Writer*

"Divinely inspired, beautifully written—a must read!"
 —*Gerald D. Benally, author of Premonition (2013)*

"*Prince Tennyson* is a sweet story that will put tears in your eyes and hope in your heart at the same time."
 —*Author Shanti Krishnamurty*

Jenni James © copyright 2019

All rights reserved as permitted under the U.S. Copyright Act of 1976. No part of this publication may be reproduced, distributed, or transmitted in any form or by any means, or stored in a database or retrieval system, without the prior permission of the publisher. The only exception is brief quotations in printed reviews.

Village Lane Publishing
Provo Utah, Idaho and Germany
www.VillageLanePublishing.com

First eBook Edition: 2013
First Paperback Edition: 2013

Second eBook Edition: 2019
Second Paperback Edition: 2019
ISBN: 978-1-951496-96-8

The characters and events portrayed in this book are fictitious. Any similarity to a real person, living or dead, is coincidental and not intended by the author.

Published in the United States of America

Village Lane Publishing, LLC

ALSO BY JENNI JAMES

Jenni James Faerie Tale Collection:
Beauty and the Beast
Sleeping Beauty
Cinderella
Snow White
Hansel and Gretel
Jack and the Beanstalk
The Frog Prince
The Twelve Dancing Princesses
Rapunzel
The Little Mermaid
Rumplestiltskin
Peter Pan
Return to Neverland
Captain Hook

The Jane Austen Diaries:
Pride & Popularity
Northanger Alibi
Persuaded
Emmalee
Mansfield Ranch
Sensible & Sensational

Prince Tennyson
Revitalizing Jane

Regency Romance Series
The Bluestocking and the Dastardly, Intolerable Scoundrel
Lord Romney's Exquisite Widow
Lord Atten Meets His Match

Modern Fairy Tales
Not Cinderella's Type
Beauty IS the Beast
Sleeping Beauty: Back to Reality
The Shattered Slipper

*This book is dedicated to my mom.
She did wonders raising her six dwarves.
Plus, she is a magical fairy grandmother.*

Snow White

CHAPTER ONE

RAVEN LAUGHED AS SHE looked across the crowded ballroom at her new sister, Snow. They were the best of friends and had been for years—now she could not believe her luck! Sisters, truly sisters—it seemed like a magical wish come true. They had imagined and dreamed of it, and it was finally a reality. Snow's father had proposed less than four months ago to Raven's mother, Queen Melantha Flynn, a beautiful, widowed woman with two children.

Not that they were still children. Corlan was nearly twenty-two and Raven and Snow were both in their late teens, but Snow's father would always consider them children. Raven watched as her beautiful new sister ran up to her, her long black curls bobbing as she came. There was not one person in Snow's kingdom who had not instantly become enamored with the girl. She had a special quality about her—a naivety and zest for life, an inner joy—something that radiated from her happy smile and wound itself about the hearts of all those who were near her.

"It has finally happened!" Snow exclaimed as she wrapped her arms around Raven and hugged her tightly.

"I know, I know! I can't believe today has come at last!"

Snow pulled back, her full red lips arching in a pretty smile against her pale skin, her black lashes fluttering briefly over her brilliant blue eyes. She was a stunning beauty. If Raven did not love her as much as she did, she would find the green tinges of jealously invading her thoughts, but as it was, she simply could not think ill of the enchanting Snow White. No one could.

"Where is Corlan?" Snow grinned. "I must hug my new brother as well."

Raven glanced over to where Corlan stood, watching them intently, his eyes never straying from Snow. He had been head over heels for the girl since they were children. Long before their parents had agreed to marry, King Herbert, Snow's father, had often brought her to play with them, the neighboring royal children, so she could experience friendship. He worried that without her mother, she would become too sad and lose the finer, elegant qualities needed to turn into a lady and ruler one day. And so he hoped to bring her out of the melancholy of losing her dear mother and into the warmth of the Flynn court.

"He is over there." Raven nodded toward her brother.

She grinned at Corlan's reaction as the stunning girl rushed toward him and threw her arms about his shoulders. He held her and closed his eyes briefly, no doubt reveling in the feel of her so close to him.

Snow pulled back, and Raven loved the way her brother's eyes observed that lively face before him, watching each movement, each smile, each word as it came from her lips.

When would he tell her he was in love? Raven had been asking him for months now, but he would never answer.

Just then, a dashing young man stepped forward and bowed low before the pretty princess in her red-and-gold gown.

"Princess Snow," Raven heard him say, "will you do me the honor of dancing the first set with me?"

Raven glanced around the grand ballroom. It would seem indeed that it was time to begin the entertainment her mother had requested. Several couples already lined the outskirts of the floor, waiting for the king and new queen to begin their nuptial dance.

"Snow is dancing with me for the first set," Corlan answered.

Raven looked over at her brother. Bravo. He stood just a bit taller, with his arm wrapped around Snow's shoulders.

Snow smiled sweetly at the man. "I promise to go out on the floor with you during the second."

The man glanced from Snow to Corlan and then back to Snow again. He must have liked the smile on her face, for he bowed lower and said, "Your Highness, there is nothing I wish for more."

She nodded, and then looked up at Corlan.

"Shall we?" he asked.

They really did make an incredible couple. Corlan was so tall and dashing, with his distinguished brown hair and lightly sun-kissed skin and deep green eyes. He was a sight to behold. But Snow, bless her heart, did not ever appear to prefer one man over the other. She seemed completely oblivious to the male species altogether—enjoying them, of course, and smiling serenely and capturing their hearts one by one. But every suitor who came to stare and try his hand for the fair princess left with a confused look on his face, for they simply did not know what to make of her. Did she not like them? Did they do something wrong? She seemed happy enough, but pushed away their advances as if they were nothing to her. Again and again, Raven watched princes from all over the continent come and try their best to woo her, but to no avail.

"King Herbert and Queen Melantha will now take the floor," the herald announced grandly.

Raven watched her mother, a stunning red-haired beauty glorious in pale-gold silk, step into the arms of her beloved Herbert as they began to waltz on the floor of the sparkling chandeliered room. The guests exclaimed over the couple as they passed by, tittering behind fans and whispering of their happiness for the great king and queen.

They had sent a surge of new hope throughout the land by uniting the two kingdoms. Raven could feel the excitement and joy buzzing through the air in pings of awareness at the exhilaration this wedding brought to all.

Raven smiled as her mother came near and then dipped and spun away as the music wound down. Even though she was in her early forties, there was no woman who could claim to have the beauty she still possessed—a vision of loveliness from her shining head of hair to her dainty, nimble feet.

The first set of dances was about to begin. Raven sighed and looked around the room, her heart clenching slightly within her chest. So many of the couples were already eagerly waiting to take their places on the dance floor. She had hoped that by now, a young man would have been inclined to ask for her hand during this particular set, today of all days when it was her mother's wedding. But no young man made his way toward her. Indeed, most of them were across the room, keenly watching Snow and Corlan speak softly and laugh with one another.

It was no use. There would never be a man who saw her while her dear new sister was in the room. Taking a deep breath, she blinked back a few tears and attempted to paste on a smile. She refused to become a silly water pot today, when everything she could have wished for came true. This was the happiest day of her life.

"Excuse me, Princess Raven Flynn?" a dashing young man asked as he walked toward her and then bowed.

Butterflies flurried wildly within her chest. "Yes?" she replied a little breathlessly. He was unbelievably handsome, with his blond hair and deep brown eyes.

"Forgive me for being so forward and not waiting for a proper introduction. I am Prince Terrance from the Sybright court and was pointed in your direction. I was wondering if you knew if the Princess Snow White was free this set? I have only just arrived, by invitation of King Herbert, and have been eager to meet this paragon I have heard mentioned."

"Oh." Her smile tightened. "Of course." She nodded, reminding herself that someone as attractive as he would only ever wish to be with Snow. "She is engaged at present," she said as the dancers began to walk upon the floor. "But if you wait your turn, she is indeed very amiable and would be more than happy to stand up with you."

"Perfect." He smiled, showing off two adorable dimples as he did so.

Raven gasped, and then quickly bit her lip to keep from doing it again. She had always longed for a man with dimples.

Terrance grinned down at her, those indentations only deepening more. "Are you perchance free at the moment?" he asked, looking around as if amazed she was still standing with him and not upon the floor.

"Yes, I am."

"And do you mean to dance?"

"Of course I do."

He took a pace back and swept another bow. "Forgive me, princess! I did not realize. Please, would you do me the honor of stepping out with me?"

She giggled. "I would be delighted," she said as she placed her hand within his and walked onto the floor.

CHAPTER TWO

PRINCE TERRANCE WAS AN expert dancer. His graceful dips and spins allowed Raven to lose herself in the moment of being in his arms. She loved to dance. How she loved feeling this freedom and joy as the world spun with her. She enjoyed dancing so very much that she would eagerly step out on the floor with anyone who asked. However, to have such an agreeable partner as this—it was magical.

A soft smile played upon her lips as the musicians finished the first song and began the introduction to the second. Each partnership always danced two dances together in a set during the Olivian balls and wedding ceremonies. It was a custom, one she was particularly grateful for at this time.

"You dance exceptionally well," Terrance said as they began the steps of the second dance.

"Thank you."

"No, thank you. I've had yet to meet such a wonderful partner. I am of a mind to keep you to myself all night long and not allow you a moment to dance with anyone else."

Her heart began to pound. "Do not be silly."

His dimples peeked out at her. "Indeed, I am not. I am as frank as I have ever been. Your dancing is unparalleled by anyone I have ever known. A good dancing partner is hard to find."

Her cheeks felt warm again and she quickly looked away, not sure how to take such compliments. There were Snow and Corlan not five feet from them.

Snow smiled and waved a gloved hand as Corlan nodded.

"Who is that beautiful girl?" Terrance asked almost reverently, his steps slowing.

With her head turned away from him, Raven closed her eyes briefly and replied, "That vision of loveliness is my new sister and dearest friend, the princess Snow White." She felt his hand clutch hers.

"So there she is! The rumors did not exaggerate her beauty at all. I have never seen such remarkable features and grace in all my life."

Raven swallowed a sudden lump in her throat before whispering, "Yes, she is unbelievably kind and generous, too. One can't help but love her."

"She *is* a paragon among women! I thought the rumors must have been exaggerated."

Her head still turned away, Raven was too emotional to speak. She only nodded as Terrance stopped dancing entirely in the center of the grand ballroom, mesmerized by the glorious girl before him.

"And look how elegant are her steps! This family has exceedingly choice dancing partners."

No, Raven thought. *There is only one exceedingly choice dancing partner in this family. And then there is one who is decidedly not choice or wanted at all.* She blinked back the rising moisture in her eyes. Goodness, this would not do. "Excuse me." She pulled away, refusing to meet his eyes. "I am suddenly very fatigued. Do you mind if we sit out the second song?"

"Are you tired?" His voice held an element of surprise. "Surely you would rather continue dancing," he said as his feet began to move again.

Carry on and know that you are only watching and coveting another partner?

"Nay." Her feet did not budge. "Forgive my rudeness, but I am not feeling well. I must leave at once." She dipped a quick curtsy and hurried off the floor before he could say another word.

Raven maneuvered around several guests as she made her way out of the grand ballroom and up quite a lot of stairs to the private wing of the castle. After a few more twists and turns, she was able to slip into her own personal rooms. They had been given to her just the week before.

Walking past the ornate canopied bed, she opted for the cream-colored chaise lounge situated beneath the large window. Not wanting to crush her gold-and-red gown—identical to Snow's—she sat carefully against the pillowed armrest. In a few minutes she would go back down to the glittering wedding party, but for now, she needed a moment, some time alone to regroup her thoughts and remind herself of all the good things in her life.

For there were many.

She dashed at a few wayward tears. Why must she insist on crying today, of all days?

She had known for years the effect Snow had on everyone. It was not something new or even worth mentioning or caring about, let alone becoming emotional over. There was nothing Raven could do. Snow would always be the sparkling, more attractive, sweet, engaging sister. Always. Raven would be the forgotten one.

There was nothing wrong with being forgotten. What girl truly wished to be the center of attention, anyway? It would be excessively awkward to know you could not make a move without another watching and deciphering your actions at all times. Who would want to live like that?

No. Raven preferred to be the one overlooked. It allowed for many times of quiet reflection, for the amusing game of people watching and clearing her head of silliness. And long moments of twiddling her thumbs and wishing to be included and hoping someone, somewhere, would find her pretty enough to enjoy her company.

Raven groaned and buried her head in her hands. *Stop this foolishness at once. Just stop. It does not change one thing and only brings on a portion of melancholy no one needs to be introduced to at this time.*

Frustrated with herself, she pushed off the chaise lounge, walked over to the carved vanity table, and sat down. Peering into the looking glass, she saw a very sullen young lady staring back at her with nondescript features. Mousy brown hair and mousy brown eyes. *No wonder people do not like you overly much,* she chided herself. *Look at the way your lips are turned down.* She forced a smile upon her face. It made a vast improvement to her features. She pinched her cheeks to bring the color back into them.

No matter how hard she tried, she would never be as beautiful as Snow, but at least she would be able to preserve a level of normalcy. So what if she never married or attracted a man? There was so much more to life than becoming a spouse. Even within her own land, there were many different ways she could become more useful—she simply needed to find them and not wither away, wondering if she would ever be included in someone's life.

Perhaps the answer was not to be included, but rather, to start her own project or idea. Then it would not be as if she was overlooked or unwanted—indeed, she would be the one to include others. And she would be sure to find all those no one else wanted and let them know they were needed too.

Smiling at her reflection, she stood up and walked out of her rooms, prepared to face the dazzling world below. But once she made it to the final landing, she needed to take a deep breath to steady her nerves before she began to step down the grand staircase that led to the ballroom.

She was surprised to see Terrance at the foot of it, pacing.

He looked at her when she approached. "Are you well?"

"Yes, thank you."

He walked up the last few steps to come back down with her. "You are sure? I did not make you ill with my confounded rudeness?"

"Your—what do you mean?"

He shook his head and clasped her hand, pausing at the end of the stairs. "Forgive me, Princess. I have thought over my actions repeatedly the last several minutes and have found them very lacking. I would like to beg a proper apology. You deserve to have the full attention of your partner and I have erred significantly in not giving it to you. Will you forgive my lack of manners and boorish ways?"

"I—uh . . ." She blinked and then promptly closed her mouth when she realized it was open. Raven did not know whether to be amazed the man thought of her enough to apologize or to be mortified that her actions made him feel the need to do so. "Goodness!" she finally said. "I do not deserve nor expect such an apology." She pulled her hand out of his and began to walk forward again, dismissing his eagerness with a flick of her wrist. "I am quite accustomed to this treatment. You can't help yourself for noticing my sister's beauty any more than anyone else can. Believe me when I say that I expect no different treatment from you than I do any other."

Terrance halted her again, once more clasping her hand. Slowly he pulled her toward him until they faced one another. His dark eyes searched hers a moment. The worry upon his brow did not allow for one dimple to peek out. *That is the true tragedy here, not my overly sensitive feelings. The man should be smiling.*

He inhaled rather sharply before saying, "The fact that you dismiss this extreme discourtesy of mine as commonplace rather sharpens the pain and adds to the weight I am bearing. Please, I beg of you to forgive me."

She met his intense gaze for several moments, wondering what else he had hidden within. "You are forgiven, but certainly, there was nothing to forgive. I am not the type to place blame upon another. I know full well my weaknesses and lack of charms. I do not expect any man to wish to be with me when my sweet sister is in the room. It is not pity I seek, or forgiveness—it is merely a fact I have learned to accept."

Terrance slowly shook his head before leaning over and leaving a very surprising, very gentle kiss upon her mouth.

CHAPTER THREE

SNOW GLANCED AROUND THE room for the third time since stepping out with her new partner. Where was Raven? It was hard to appear fully lost in Lord Loland's continual prattle whilst covertly searching for her sister. The last time she had seen Raven was upon the dance floor, smiling up at that charming man and completely oblivious to anyone else.

Snow grinned. Could it be that Raven was finally losing her heart to someone? Snow looked again and did not see the tall young man her stepsister had been dancing with either. Perhaps they were together. Oh, goodness! After all these years, was there at last a gentleman who could see what Snow saw? If so, she would love him forever herself. How many times did she push the silly princes and men of the court away, hoping one of them would turn around and see the glories that made Raven?

Yet none of them did.

Curse this silly enchantment, anyway. It *had* to be an enchantment—though no one else claimed to know anything about it, there was no other logical reason for the attention she received. It was folly. Snow sighed. For once she would like to be seen for herself and not because of a spell.

"I beg your pardon," Lord Loland said. "Am I boring you with my endless talk? I did not mean to make you sigh."

Oh, dear. "No. It was not you. It was—" How does one rectify sighing while dancing with one's partner?

Thankfully, the song ended.

"Your Royal Majesties, prince and princesses, lords and ladies of the court," the herald began, "it is with pleasure that I direct your attention to King Herbert and Queen Melantha as they open the royal gifts they are bestowing upon one another. These are the only presents that will be opened publicly, though they would like to thank their guests who did bring gifts of their appreciation for the marriage. For now, may you enjoy the festivities and the customs of Olivian. King Herbert and Queen Melantha." He swept his arm toward the couple seated upon ornately carved high-backed chairs as the crowd surged forward.

Snow headed for the seats reserved for her and her new siblings. Glancing over, she watched as Raven walked in on the arm of the handsome gentleman she had been dancing with earlier. Her heart burst with happiness at the sight—it most definitely seemed as though Raven had found someone. She caught her sister's eye and motioned her forward.

Raven turned and pulled away from the man's arm, speaking a few words to him before she came and sat with Snow.

"Hello," Snow said. "Have you been enjoying yourself?"

Raven rolled her eyes. "There is nothing going on with anything or anyone."

Snow laughed. "You sound like a girl trying to convince herself. He appears to be a very nice man. Who is he?"

"He is a very nice man—too nice, really. His name is Prince Terrance of the Sybright court and he has traveled this whole way to make your acquaintance."

Good heavens. Snow sat back in her chair. "Another?"

Raven looked out toward the gathering crowd. Almost everyone was situated. "Just so."

"I would prefer not to meet him, then." Snow sighed. Why must every eligible man come to her? It was not fair.

"I believe it will be inevitable. It would seem he was invited by your father specifically to be introduced to you."

"Father? He would not dare!"

"He already has."

"What has Father done?" Corlan asked as he sat down next to the girls.

"Invited another suitor for Snow," Raven explained.

Snow watched Corlan's jaw twitch. "Another one?"

"I am not any happier about it than you are." Snow folded her arms. "Why would he think to do something like this? It forces me to want to run away. If he just left things as they are, he might find himself attending my wedding soon. But to be forever plaguing me with men and allowing all those who wish to see me to do so—I find it completely…" She trailed off when she realized she had been speaking a bit louder than was seemly.

The king and queen were just about to begin opening their gifts when Raven leaned over and whispered, "Do not throw this one away, Snow. He is different."

She looked at her sister. *How much did it cost her pride to say such a thing to me?* He must be quite a prince indeed if her sister was willing for her to give him a second glance. Snow shook her head. "No. I will not give him any more of a chance than I have the rest," she whispered back. "I deserve a man who will fall in love with the real me."

"He is more than likely the one you seek, then."

"Ahem." Corlan scowled at them both.

Snow tucked her hand through the crook of his elbow and leaned into him. "Are you tired of hearing us blather on about silliness?"

"No." His gaze met hers. "I am tired of you taking it all so seriously. There is no reason for anyone to be thinking of falling in love just yet."

"There is not?"

"No. Not until you fully know your own heart and what you truly wish. Until then, this is all a nonsensical game."

"And what do you know about falling in love?" She chuckled.

"I know a lot more than you give me credit for." He looked away.

She watched his lashes for a moment and then ran her gaze to his nose, down to his lips and then chin and jaw.

"What are you doing?" he said from the corner of his mouth.

Snow put her head onto his shoulder, still clasping his arm. "I do not know. I was just watching you for a moment. Can I not watch you?"

There was a long pause before Corlan said quietly, "I would never wish to interrupt any activity of yours that you enjoy. If it is watching me, very well, you may do so."

She grinned and squeezed his arm a bit tighter. He really was such a wonderful older brother.

Melantha's lady-in-waiting approached with her father's gift.

Just then Raven gasped.

Snow glanced over at her and then toward their parents, where Raven was looking.

Oh, my word! What is Father thinking? "Tell me I am not seeing the Lythereon Mirror being presented to Melantha. Even if he doesn't believe in the rumors, tell me Father would not have thought to do something as ludicrous as that."

"Does he not understand the curse associated with that thing?" Corlan asked, his foot tapping upon the ground. "Foolish gift!"

"Mother has wanted that mirror for years. She has always thought she could save the world with it. And hoping to impress her, King Herbert has obviously granted her the wish of her heart," Raven said. "Look at her smile, the joy on her face."

Snow could not stop staring at the genuine giddiness Melantha displayed as she had two footmen hold the mirror up so she could admire herself. "Why would anyone want that particular looking glass?" When Raven and Corlan did not answer, she continued, "Perhaps there is nothing to worry about. Perhaps the legends are false and it is merely just a mirror and nothing more."

Corlan squeezed her hand. "And perhaps Snow has read too many fairy stories and believes that everything is always perfect."

"What is the worst that could happen to us?" she asked him.

"The mirror is evil, pure evil, and will bring out the vilest thoughts of any who possess it. It is also said to make them extremely powerful."

"So, if that legend is true," Raven said slowly, speaking aloud the fears neither of them were willing to voice, "how long until we lose our mother completely to the control of the mirror?"

CHAPTER FOUR

"SNOW," HER FATHER CALLED out from the west drawing room as she headed up the grand staircase. "Come in here a moment—I would like you to meet someone."

Snow paused at the second step, knowing it really was inevitable—she would have to meet Prince Terrance. She turned and smiled at her father, who was standing just inside the door as she came into the fashionably decorated green-and-white room. "Yes?" Her gaze focused solely on her father, not the man she could see from the corner of her eye seated in Melantha's favorite chair about eight feet away.

Herbert wrapped his arm around her shoulder and turned her toward the handsome man as he stood up. "Prince Terrance wrote me and requested a visit some time ago. I replied to the missive, as I felt it necessary that you two meet. He is of the Sybright court, which was, until recently, run by his father, the late King Alexander II. Now his mother is on the throne until he can find a suitable woman to marry and make her his queen. Alexander and I were schoolmates years ago and the best of friends. I, of course, welcome any of his family into my home, and I hope you will go out of your way to guarantee that Terrance is treated with the greatest courtesy and respect."

Snow curtsied and met the prince's eyes. He was probably one of the more handsome men who had come to try his hand with her. When he smiled and bowed low, she knew why Raven was so smitten by him—dimples. How many times had Raven exclaimed over wanting a husband with dimples?

Her father continued, "Prince Terrance, may I present my fair daughter, the delightfully captivating princess Snow White? She is my only child by birth and holds a very special place in my heart. She is goodness itself—kind and thoughtful, with a lively mind and caring soul."

Snow tried not to grimace as she looked over at her father. The fine lines around his eyes creased as he spoke of her. She loved him so very much, but there were days when he could mortify her.

He grinned and kissed her forehead. "Now stop blushing so much, my dear, and shake hands with the poor man. He has traveled days to be here." He gently pushed her toward him.

Snow held out her hand and enjoyed the prince's firm, yet careful, hold. "Hello," she said, her gaze meeting his. "I hope you find everything you are looking for here in Olivian and will go home a very happy man."

"Only time will tell. I await these next six weeks with fervent hope that what you say may come true."

Those dark brown eyes danced a moment, and she could not tell if he knew she was speaking of Raven or if he believed her to be speaking of herself. Whichever the answer, he did seem to have a maturity about him—he had an older soul than any of the other suitors who had come before. He *was* different.

She tilted her head slightly and smiled—*genuinely* smiled this time. "Thank you. I believe we shall *all* have fun getting to know one another."

He watched that smile and inhaled sharply as if he were reacting to whatever enchantment she had about her.

Snow's face fell. No—he could not decide upon her for his wife. Not until he saw Raven again. *There is no future with me; there never will be for any man until dear Raven is happily settled.*

"Father?" She turned toward him. "Since the prince has planned to stay with us for so long, do you mind if I introduce him to Corlan and Raven as well? I believe we shall all get along famously."

"Of course! I would expect nothing less. He is staying in the guest quarters and should be treated as one of the family as much as possible."

"Then I shall take him to the library, where they both are at present." She glanced over. "If that is well with you?"

Terrance hesitated a fraction before stating, "Yes. Thank you."

"If you will follow me?" There was no reason to stay another moment in the drawing room. "Good night, Father." She kissed his cheek. "The wedding was beautiful, and your bride even more so."

"Aye, it has been a wonderful day. I will leave you to explore and get to know one another." He grinned and waggled his eyebrows at her. "I have a new bride to attend to."

Snow laughed and kissed his other cheek. "I will see you in the morning."

She walked out of the room and waited at the staircase for Terrance before ascending. Together they began to climb.

"Princess Snow," he began, "I can see you are not completely in favor of me coming to meet you. Is there a reason I am not to your liking, or is there something else I should know? Something you refuse to speak of and yet I can see hiding in the depths of your very stunning blue eyes?"

"My!" She was shocked. "You do get right to the point, do you not?"

He chuckled as they turned at the landing and continued up. "I know I have been frank. I am driven to do what is right, and I find that honesty and being completely upfront from the beginning always work best in my dealings. And so, I ask you again, is there something I should know? Something you would like to discuss prior to meeting your new sister and brother?"

Holding out her arm, she stopped him before they made their way down the wide corridor that led to the library. Turning to him, she asked, "Can I trust you?"

He matched her gaze steadily with his own before replying, "I believe so."

"I have much I wish to impart and no one to share it with. And here you are, like a godsend, asking me to reveal to you what is in my heart. It is indeed a very tempting proposition, though I fear you will not be happy with me once it is all out."

He shook his head and stepped forward. "Princess Snow, I am not the type to judge wrongly or to entertain false hopes. I thrive in knowing the situation from the beginning. If you mean to use me as a confidant of some sort, as long as you are not planning murder" –he paused to grin— "know that I will heed your wishes and allow you to speak without revealing what you have told me to a soul."

He had such calmness about him. "Are you sure you are not a knight of King Arthur's court come back to life?"

Chuckling, he replied, "I wish! I fear I am not half as noble or own a portion of the integrity they did. But men like that are truly my heroes."

Snow liked him. It made absolutely no sense at all to trust him as she did, but she knew she could. "Very well. You have won me over. I shall take the risk and make you my confidant, though you must promise to be my friend no matter what I reveal."

CHAPTER FIVE

TERRANCE WATCHED SNOW TAKE a deep breath and then say, "Come here. There is not much time." She led him to a small alcove in the corridor. It was a window seat with views overlooking a large portion of the kingdom.

Once they both were sitting on the plush cushions, she earnestly began, "I have told no one, but I fear I am under a spell to make people love me. You are only one of many hundreds—*hundreds*—who have come to pay court to me. It is exasperating and confusing and frustrating, the attention I receive. I wish to be normal and loved for who I am, not simply because every single man in my vicinity can look at nothing else. I do not know how to break this, either. It is terrifying and I secretly worry it will be my demise one day."

"I see." His eyes roamed over her features. She was extremely beautiful—easily the most beautiful woman he had ever seen. But was that enough to capture the hearts and attention of every single man she had ever met? It may be. But she could be correct in assuming there was something cast upon her, for he did feel an undeniable tug that he had never felt toward anyone before.

She continued, "It seems to affect women as well—not in the same way, but thankfully they like me and are not overly jealous as of yet. But I fear one of them will be able to remove herself from my enchantment sooner or later and then desire me dead."

"Why would they want you dead?"

"Because of the attention I receive, of course. It can't be pleasing to any female to watch another be lauded with all the glory. Take Raven, for instance. She is a very pretty girl and should have her own onslaught of suitors, and yet, no man will look twice at her. I genuinely fear they never will while I am still here and unwed."

"Then why have you not done so?" he asked, confused at her logic. If she truly cared for Raven, why not accept one of the hundreds of men vying for her hand?

She sighed and gave him a look that showed what a simpleton she thought him. "Because I want a man to love *me*—the *real* me. And I can't guarantee that anyone knows the real me with this spell attached. Besides, I vowed long ago that I would not entertain any suitors until Raven was wed."

"Are you jesting? You would put your life on hold, hoping someone would wed her first, when you yourself say it is impossible to notice your sister?"

"No, I am not jesting. I am determined to do just that. She is a delight. She is my best friend. And she has been passed over and left behind again and again, and I can't have her go last in this as well. She deserves happiness as much as anyone."

"You really do have a large heart."

"I love her that much. She has done so many things for me. But I can't let her know how I feel or she would be livid."

"I can imagine that much." He cleared his throat and then said, "Can I reveal something to you?"

"Yes."

Was he a fool to tell her? Perhaps it would help her to know. "I kissed Princess Raven today."

"You did what?"

"It was a very pleasant surprise for us both, but yes, I did kiss her."

"Terrance!" Her face was wreathed in smiles. "I am so happy to hear such news! You have made this the most perfect day, even more perfect than before."

"She slapped me."

Snow's smile dropped. "I beg your pardon?"

"No, do not. It was warranted. I should not have shocked her as I did. But she was so matter-of-fact and forlorn and adorable, I had to lean down and kiss her."

"But she slapped you?"

"Yes. Quite soundly. She has a forceful hand, that one."

"Oh, dear."

He grinned. "It did not put me off at all. In fact, it had me wishing to come into her good graces even more." After Raven had slapped him, he would not allow her to walk into the ballroom until she was smiling again.

"Terrance, are you saying what I think you are saying?" she asked.

"I am definitely astounded by the events of today," he hedged. "I came to this palace for the sole purpose of meeting you and before I could do so, I had quite outrageously ruined any chances I might have had with that rather fetching sister of yours."

"I do not believe they are ruined, per se."

"Oh, of course not. There is nothing a man loves more than a worthy challenge. And finding a delightful, forgotten minx in the process may prove to be exactly what my heart needs. However, she has become cynical and believed herself to be worthless for a long while. It will take persistence on my part, and going very slowly with her."

"Are you truly going to try for her hand?"

"I admit to feeling a strong pull to you when I saw you and again when we met. It is there, but after speaking to you and hearing your fears, I have to wonder where my true loyalties lie. I believe my interest, for whatever reason, has already been claimed."

"Perhaps it is because you met her first and spent time with her before you met me."

He thought about it and then shrugged. "Perhaps."

She grinned. "Would you like to see her again?"

Was he ready to see Raven so soon? "Is there anything else plaguing you?" he asked Snow instead of answering her question.

"Yes, but it can wait. This is much more exciting."

His heart began to beat strangely within his chest. "You know, I believe you may be right."

"You will soon learn that a woman is always right, and a royal princess more so than any other."

"My word. You females were definitely sent to cause us a merry chase."

"Yes, but it is worth it. Now, let us go find them." She stood up. "You will love Corlan. He is without a doubt one of the most engaging people you will ever meet. They are my dearest friends and always will be."

He walked with Snow down the long corridor. She prattled on about the qualities of her new siblings, but he was not attending as his own mind raced. What if he was mistaken? What if Raven was not the one for him? What if he met her again and saw that his impulses had forced him to react in pity instead of with growing interest? He was a tad frightened to walk into the room and see a rather drab, boring girl before him. There was one thing he knew for certain—he required a lively mind to accompany him for eternity, for he could never be satisfied with a meek mouse. And if she was often overlooked and forgotten, perhaps it was because she was quiet and shy.

It was then that he remembered the slap upon his cheek and smiled. She was certainly no mouse! However, he needed to be cautious about what he revealed to either sister. It was wrong of him to allow Snow's hopes to become carried away. He desired to approach Raven slowly to see if she did have all the qualities he preferred, and if so, he wanted to gain her trust and admiration so he might claim her hand.

Why in the world was it so hard to court a woman these days? Good heavens, they should resort back to matchmaking—so much less messy that way.

Snow stopped at a doorway and called in, "Corlan? Raven? Are you still here?"

CHAPTER SIX

RAVEN GLANCED UP FROM the book she was reading. "Yes, come in," she replied. Her heart jumped at the sight of Terrance walking in with Snow. He was such a handsome man! She dropped the book. Goodness, it should be a crime to have a face like that. Glancing at Snow's features and then the contrast of her hair color to his lighter blond—it was indeed quite striking. They made an incredibly beautiful couple.

She sighed and picked up the book. Never mind. He had finally met Snow and therefore should not be considered worth her time in contemplating his good looks, for they would never be turned in her direction again.

She flushed when she thought of his kiss earlier. How soft and thrilling it had been, and so unexpected! Grimacing slightly, she raised the book higher to cover her features. And to believe she slapped him afterward. But it was so shocking and forward—what else was she to do? Kiss him again, as any other sensible girl in her shoes would have done. She let out a little moan of regret and reminded herself once more that none of it mattered—he would be kissing Snow's lips soon. Besides, after such a display, he would never wish to kiss Raven a second time. Perhaps that was the best protection for her heart—keeping him at such a distance that it would not matter if he fell for Snow.

"Hello again." Terrance's deep voice caused her to jump.

She peeked around the book and was amazed to find him kneeling on the floor next to her chair. "What are you doing down there?"

"I came to see you. And since you were so preoccupied with that book, I decided the best thing would be to join you." He pulled on the pages. "What are you reading?"

"I, uh…" Great mercy! It was upside down!

"I hear it is easier to read them this way." He chuckled near her ear and then flipped the book around for her.

"Thank you," she muttered.

He laughed louder. "So, if you were not reading, what exactly *were* you doing?"

"Nothing. Go away, you bothersome man."

"No. For there is nothing more entertaining to a bothersome man than to find the exact girl he hopes to bother hiding from him."

She met his dark eyes. Why was he next to her, and looking at her with such a playful gaze? He could not possibly be interested in anything but tormenting her.

Right? She glanced over to see Snow and Corlan discussing the book on travels he had procured earlier. Her eyes met Terrance's again. There was definitely a sparkle in their depths. She watched as his grin deepened, exposing those dimples. "What do you want?" she asked with a small smile of her own.

"Merely to say hello. Must I have ulterior motives to speak with you?"

"Well, one would continuously wonder if you did."

"Since I have none, should I leave, then? Would you prefer that more?" He stood up.

"No!" She reached for his hand and clasped it before realizing the spectacle she was making of herself. "Oh, never mind. Leave, then—I do not care."

He knelt back down. "You are quite fetching when you tell a falsehood."

My goodness! She blushed and then groaned. "Heaven save me. Of all the silly things to say…" She trailed off when she noticed how close he was.

"Yes?" he asked, his eyes staring intently at her lips.

She licked those lips and blushed again. "Why are you here? I know you do not like me one bit."

"Not one bit? Are you sure?" A dimple peeked out.

All at once Raven could not breathe at all. His nearness, his looks, his warm, rich voice … all of it collided with her senses to cause her to react in a most peculiar way. If she was not careful, she would begin to believe this silliness. He was clearly using her as a pawn of some sort—he could not be serious in his attentions. In a flurry of motion, she stood up and walked blindly over to a bookshelf at random to put away the book in her hand and fetch another. That should have been a very simple task, and one that did not take much brain power to accomplish, but Terrance followed her like a lion stalking the frightened lamb.

"Why do you run from me?" he asked.

She sighed after searching through several titles and not reading one of them. Turning around, she said, "Why do you follow me?"

"Because I am curious about you."

"But do you not see that I wish you as far away from me as possible?"

"That is what you are trying to make me believe." He reached over and captured a long ringlet in his hand.

Her breath caught as his knuckles brushed against her neck.

"But it is *that* reaction which tells me you are lying. Why would you lie to me?" he asked.

"I am not lying! Stop saying that. I would never tell a falsehood—I honestly do not wish to have you near. Your touch alarms me."

She watched a spark of pain flicker across his features before he nodded and pulled back, dropping the lock of hair. "Forgive my forward manners."

Was he sincerely interested in her? Raven's heart lurched as he began to walk away. "Terrance, wait!" She spoke in a rush.

He glanced back.

"I, uh—" She licked her lips again. "I am afraid of you." Great heavens, could she sound a bigger fool?

"Why?"

She was not sure she could answer him. *Because you will hurt me too much. I know it. I know deep down inside that if I let my guard down and begin to imagine the possibility of you, it will harm me more than if I keep you away from me forever.*

"Raven?" he asked, turning more fully toward her. When she did not respond, he whispered, "I find you slightly terrifying as well, and your words and actions confuse me into being something I am not. If I am completely honest, at this moment I wish to wrap you up in my arms and kiss you again."

When she gasped, he grinned.

"'Tis true. I wish to see if your lips really feel as wonderful as I remember, or if my mind is wreaking havoc with my memories. And yet, I am scared to touch one who does not wish to have anything to do with me. I hope it is because you are fearful of being injured and not because you actually believe me to be a hideous person. But I stand here battling within myself over a girl I hardly know, wondering if she could find me as interesting as I find her."

Raven could not believe this was happening. Her first reaction was to run as fast as she could, but thankfully, her traitorous feet would not budge. Was he someone she could rely upon? "Are you not attracted to Snow?" she asked.

"Of course I am," he answered, piercing her heart. "But I find myself attracted to you more."

"You—you do?" Out of nowhere, butterflies exploded in her stomach.

"Yes?"

"But why?"

He stepped slowly toward her. "Because you fascinate me, and it has been a very long time since anyone has. Though your sister is lovely, you are the more interesting prize and therefore the one I can't stop thinking about."

"You will change your mind. You will wake up from this and run away, shouting down the hills."

He chuckled, which made her laugh as well. "Perhaps," he answered too truthfully. "I could very well run away this moment. But for now, I am eager to see where this goes, and willing to wait a bit longer to decide if I shall run or not."

"But what if I run from you?"

Those dimples deepened as he closed the distance between them. "My dear girl, you already are. Which may be why I like you so much." He then leaned down and kissed her once gently on the mouth.

CHAPTER SEVEN

SNOW LOOKED UP JUST in time to watch Terrance kiss Raven as she and Corlan rounded the corner. She nudged Corlan with her elbow. "Do you see them?" she whispered, excitement bubbling within her.

"Oh," was all he said, staring at his sister with his mouth slightly open.

"Is it not brilliant? I think they make a charming couple."

"I thought he was here for you."

"Well, apparently he *came* for me, but met Raven first." She pulled him to a settee out of the way. "Come and sit with me."

"Oh," he said again. Corlan slowly joined Snow on the small couch.

Snow glanced at him and was startled to find him staring at her. "What is it?"

"He is a very handsome man. Are you sure you do not wish him to be enamored with you?"

A sudden desire to thump Corlan overcame her. "Why would you say anything so inane? I do wish for my sister to have happiness too, you know. Besides, I am not looking to find any man at present, remember?"

"Yes, but . . ."

"But what? You, yourself, commented earlier how you wish I would not take this all so seriously."

"I know, and I do. But I have to wonder just what it is you are looking for in a man."

She blinked. "Nothing, Corlan. I do not want a man currently."

"Yes, but if you did, what characteristics would you wish him to have?"

She sighed. He had never acted so odd before. "Very well. I have not thought about it overly much, but I guess he would have to be kind."

"And?"

"It would help if he could handle a sword as well as you do." She grinned and nudged him again. "Then I would know he could keep me safe."

"Well, that is crossed out, then. No one can swordfight as well as I can."

She playfully pouted. "A girl can still hope someone will come along who could."

"Ha!" His eyes searched hers a moment before he asked, "What else would you prefer?"

She scrunched her nose and then said, "Perhaps if he could sing."

"Sing?" Corlan looked like he would die of an apoplexy right then and there.

"What?" She chuckled at his expression.

"Good grief, woman! You can't be serious! This is your list? This is who you hope to win your hand in marriage?" He ticked them off with his fingers. "A man who is kind, can swordfight, and *sing?*"

"Well, you should not have asked if you did not want to hear the answer."

"I just can't believe the simplicity of the answer. Where are the other qualities? Like, a man who is loyal? A man who will put your needs before his own? A man who would face all of Hades to hold your hand? A man who wishes to kiss you thoroughly and keep you safe next to his heart every night?"

He continued to count. "A man who can't wait to hear what words you speak next because you mesmerize him so much, a man who wishes to be better just because he knows you believe in him and love him, a man who wants to raise a family with you so he can see those little children grow and laugh and play and enchant the world the same as their mother."

His voice grew a bit softer. "A man who needs you to live because if you were gone, his world would be over. A man, a true man, who loves and laughs and lives and breathes. A man who is a part of the world—not merely coasting with it, but making his mark to change it for good.

"Where is this man?" he whispered. "Where are your dreams of him?"

Snow's breathing became so labored, she did not realize the tears had begun to fall until one plopped upon her hand. Glancing down, she stared at the sparkling drop until another joined its place.

"Snow?"

"Yes?" She looked up, but her eyes were swimming with tears and he blurred before her. Quickly she dashed them away.

"Have I upset you?"

"No." She shook her head. "Not at all. I did not know such a creature existed. I would not allow myself to hope for such a man before now."

"He exists. You will have to open your eyes to see him, though."

"What if I can't? What if I miss him?"

"He will not let you."

His steady, confident gaze did much to confirm that his words were sincere. "What would I do without you?" she asked.

He grinned a bit ruefully and looked away. "I worry you will be quite fine."

"You worry?"

His hand came up and brushed aside a strand of hair from her forehead. "All these years have allowed me to grow very fond of you. Of course I worry what it would be like if you were married to another and no longer by my side whenever I wished it."

She had not thought of that. Her brow furrowed. What would she do without Corlan? Though Raven was her best friend, Corlan was her steady voice of reason, the one person who did not cater to her every whim or believe she was perfection. Indeed, he was her pillar of strength. Not having him near would be as foreign as the sky not having the clouds or sun. She shook her head. "Then I will never marry because I need you, too."

Corlan gasped, his eyes searching hers. "Snow, what did you say?"

"I do not want to be without you. If my marriage would place a wedge between us, it is yet another reason not to attach myself to any man. You are so much a part of me, I take it for granted."

"No matter what the future holds for us, we will still be friends. I will not leave you wholly. I would not be able to treat you the same if you married another, but it does not mean you will lose me completely. Snow, despite my wishes on the matter, you should always follow your heart and choose the man *you* feel would be the best for you."

She groaned. "I can't think of such things right now."

"Then let us speak of something else."

"Please?" She smiled. "What would you like to talk about?"

"Probably the one thing we would be best to remove from our minds altogether, yet neither of us can since it will weigh constantly upon our thoughts."

What does he mean? She met his gaze and then it hit her. "Oh! The mirror."

"Yes."

"What should we do? Is there anything we *can* do? Is there a book here that could help us?"

"I hope to read everything I can on the subject. And I hope and pray it does not affect her as the legends say."

"Are you speaking of the Lythereon Mirror?" asked Raven from across the room.

Snow looked up to see Terrance and Raven watching them. "Yes. We are attempting to decide if there is anything we can do to protect Mother from it."

"Wait a moment." Terrance approached. "Do you mean to tell me your family is in possession of the Lythereon Mirror?"

Raven walked up to the group as well. "Did you not see the gift my mother opened from King Herbert?"

"Yes, but I would have never imagined it to be that cursed looking glass. Are you certain?" He looked at each of them, his hand unconsciously reaching for a sword that was not there.

Snow nodded. "My father doesn't believe in curses and he would have never presented such a gift to her if it was not the exact thing she wanted."

"Oh, my word," Terrance whispered as he glanced at Raven.

Snow could tell he was concerned about leaving Raven to face such a mess on her own, and yet wished he was anywhere but in this castle.

"Precisely," Corlan stated. "We are all very apprehensive."

"Do you believe she will hang it here in the castle?" Snow asked.

Raven sat down on the sofa next to Snow. "Where else would she put such a beloved gift?"

Snow folded her arms, the heaviness in her chest doubling. "That will make everything dashed awkward for us."

"Not just awkward. It will be much worse than that!" Terrance exclaimed.

"'Tis true," Corlan said. "If that mirror resides in the castle with us, we are all doomed."

CHAPTER EIGHT

CORLAN SLAMMED THE ANCIENT book shut as he sat upon his bed. He watched as a small cloud of dust rose from the book. It would seem the mirror was completely unbreakable. The only person who could possibly break it was the person to whom it belonged. Anyone else who attempted to destroy it would be sucked within its realm and either lose their life or become a servant of the looking glass.

If it could not be smashed, that would explain why the thing still existed.

The legend went on to say that those who owned it became so engrossed with its power and the new freedom they experienced that they would never destroy it. They became so obsessed that they could not fathom life without it. Every single owner of the mirror to date had died protecting it—prostrating themselves over the looking glass, guaranteeing it would not be harmed, forgetting, of course, that it could not be, except by them.

Corlan tossed the heavy tome upon his dresser and walked over to the window. His mother had heard tales of the mirror when she was a little girl and had always been enthralled by them. He remembered her reciting the legend of the mirror almost reverently to him and Raven when they were children. His mother used to jest that she would become the first female ruler of the mirror and would change the world with it.

What fool would have sold that mirror to King Herbert?

No, that was unfair. Anyone hoping to make a profit from an unwise king would certainly have sold it. The true question was, how could his mother and new father be so oblivious that they would ignore all the warnings associated with it and add it to their collection?

This was madness.

His eyes hurt from the hours of reading the different reports. He glanced over at the stack of books next to his bed. If the stories were to be believed, as soon as his mother hung up the mirror, it would awaken to her and everything would change from that moment on. Bad luck would befall their enemies. Bizarre calamities would need to be addressed immediately, such as natural disasters, disease outbreaks, and war that would decimate her enemies. Though the owner of the mirror would always be victorious, it would come at quite a cost to the people around them. Many of their subjects would die due to the odd occurrences.

The owner of the mirror would become irrational, power crazed, and slowly show signs of mental illness. His mother had certainly never mentioned this aspect of the mirror. The stories varied depending on the account. Some of the mirror's owners took a few years to lose their wits completely, while others began to show signs of lunacy very early on. In two instances, they were proclaimed incapable of rational thought within the first week.

Corlan had decided the night before that he would have to break the mirror himself and stop this mess, which was why he had been searching through the ancient book to find a solution. However, after reading the different firsthand accounts, he was even more worried now than when he began.

Why would his mother risk so much to do something so completely selfish?

He pushed away from the window. Not one of the stories said that the mirror protected the families and those living near the empowered being. As far as he could tell, many of the family members lost their lives, along with those in the kingdom.

It was time he paid his mother a visit to hopefully get her to see reason before it was too late.

The king had left earlier that morning to take care of some farms in the eastlands, so Corlan knew his mother was alone. He hesitated a moment outside her rooms before knocking upon the door.

"Yes?" she called.

"It is I, Corlan."

"Oh! Come in, dear!" she exclaimed. "Come in and see what I have done."

He opened the door and walked in. His mother was across the room with her back to him and beckoned him over with her hand.

"You must see this! Look. Is it not the most beautiful thing you have ever beheld?"

It took a moment for him to discover she was not wholly ignoring him as he approached—she was watching him through the new looking glass upon her wall. The mirror had her so transfixed that she would not even welcome her son properly.

With a feeling of dread, he came to stand next to her. "So you have done it. You have hung the Lythereon Mirror."

"Yes!" She giggled and clapped her hands, her gaze admiring its intricately carved wooden frame.

He had never seen her behave in such an undignified manner before.

"Is it not the most fascinating thing?" she asked. Slowly she turned from side to side, admiring her slender figure. Indeed, her whole person seemed to be even more attractive when one looked at her through the looking glass. Corlan could not dismiss the fact that her copper hair shone with more brilliancy, her blue gown had a richness to it—almost as if it had not been worn before—and her skin glowed with a luster he had never known.

"I am alluring," she whispered. "This mirror makes me the loveliest woman who ever was." Nudging him with her elbow, her eyes never leaving the reflection, she asked, "Do I not look like a girl of nineteen or twenty?"

"Aye, you do."

"Is it not captivating?"

This was not how he expected this conversation to go. "Mother, it is an illusion. It is not real. There is no reason to be captivated by such trickery."

"Look! You appear the exact same as you always do. Only I have changed in the mirror."

Corlan looked at himself and blinked. She was correct. Not that it mattered overly much if he did appear different, but it would certainly imply that the legend was true and the mirror was already showing its power. "How long has this been upon the wall?"

"I had the footmen hang it for me just now, about five minutes before you came in."

Only five minutes? He must remove it at once, before she had a chance to awaken it. As hastily as possible, he stepped in front of her and began to pull it down.

"No!" she shouted.

The thing would not budge. He yanked again. "Yes, Mother. This is evil. It is cursed and will ruin us all. I love you too much—we must remove it."

"Corlan, enough! I do not care if you are my son; I will kill you if you take it off the wall."

Amazed, he brought his arms down and turned around, blocking his mother from seeing her reflection. "What did you say?"

Her eyes blazed wildly. "You heard correctly, though if it bears repeating, I will do so."

"Mother, it has already affected you. Do you not see how possessive you have become? The legends are true! This mirror will drive you to madness. It will destroy you!"

She put her hands on her hips. "I fully understand the legends. I have always known of the power this particular looking glass possesses, but I do not for one moment believe it is affecting me! I will not allow it. I'm too strong for the mirror to affect me. It is an object, Corlan, something upon my wall."

Waving her hand for him to move, she continued, "I have wanted the Lythereon Mirror since I was a girl. It has been my dearest wish to own it and use it for good to help change this world. You know this! I have told you of my dreams countless times. Yet now, when I finally have it hanging upon my wall, you want to take it down? You, my son, are the one who has become possessive and mad. Not I."

He was about to speak when he noticed green mist coming from the frame of the mirror. "What is that?"

"Mirror?" His mother pushed him aside completely. "Mirror? Are you attempting to speak to me?"

"Do not talk to it!"

"Hush, Corlan. Silence yourself or leave this room immediately." The green mist continued to pour out onto the ground. "Mirror?" Melantha's fingers reached out and played with the smoke. It twirled about her hand and wound up her arm.

"Mother!" He wanted to pull her away but found himself frozen, completely unable to move his body.

And then he watched in growing fascination and horror as the green mist rose from the ground and completely enveloped her, twisting and winding itself around his mother from her feet to the tips of her hair. It covered her in a mystical green glow.

His jaw locked and his breathing became labored. Slowly he felt his airways closing before him as his mother chanted in an eerie voice he did not recognize.

"Mirror, mirror, on the wall.

What splendor have ye provided us all?

Here we be, both good and proud,

Wise man, foolish man, the brave and the cowed.

'Tis I who stands by the glass

Thine utmost exemplar to be at last.

Ye with all thy wisdom foresee,
And remember—give the glory to me."

CHAPTER NINE

CORLAN PULLED SNOW INTO the library and put the large book of legends back where it went. "I am telling you, it was the most terrifying thing I have ever witnessed."

"It sounds like it was!" she exclaimed, still speaking in a hushed tone. "Did the mirror converse with her?"

"Yes!" He looked around the room. Seeing they were completely alone, he walked her to the furthest point from the door, yet positioned himself so he would know if anyone came in. "There I was, frozen, not able to move, and the mirror came to life. A man's head could be seen speaking with my mother—it was not her reflection at all! My ears were shut off and I could not make out what was being said, but I am telling you, whatever it was, my mother has not been the same since."

"Yes, I said hello to her a few moments ago and she gave me a look that would have shot daggers if it could." She clutched his arm. "What should we do?"

"I do not know. I will try to ascertain what exactly is happening to her, what lunacy is beginning to control her mind so we may discern what she plans to do. But, Snow, I warn you now—do not ever go into her quarters again. Do not do it."

He paused as a maid came into the library and put a small book upon a shelf. She curtsied at the couple, but quickly went on her way.

"When I was finally released from the bizarre enchantment the mirror placed over me, I collapsed to the ground. It took several deep breaths before I was well enough again to walk out of there."

"Corlan, no! Do not say such things. I can't bear to hear of you experiencing this."

"I am fine, truly. However, until we can come up with a better solution, it is best that you and Raven stay clear of her completely. Do not even be tempted to take a peek at that mirror. I worry about the evil it controls."

She nodded before her wide eyes grew more concerned. "Corlan, I am so sorry this is happening to Melantha. How difficult for you to face. 'Tis not fair."

"No, it is not, though I worry for your father as well. Herbert is a good man, and from the legends I read, almost every spouse of those who owned the mirror were killed."

She gasped and covered her mouth.

He could have kicked himself for being such a fool. Why would he say such a thing to her? That was the absolute worst thing to reveal at such a time. "Snow, I am sorry. Forgive me—I should not have let that slip."

"Nay." She shook her head, blinking.

He could tell the emotions were too much for her. Good heavens, now he had made her cry. Such a charming prince had never existed before. "I am a dunce!"

"You are not. I need to hear the truth no matter how painful it is. If I am not aware of what is actually happening around me, how will I be able to prepare for it?"

Seeing her blue eyes shimmering with tears, he could not help himself. "Snow, I vow I will not let him die. I will protect your father at all costs."

She smiled and stood up on tiptoe. Tugging his arm toward her, she pulled his large frame down to meet her much smaller one and then, surprisingly, kissed his cheek. "Thank you," she whispered. "I will be forever in your debt."

The mirror's dark magic must have done more to Corlan's brain than he realized, for in the next second, he clasped her shoulders and kissed her upon those full red lips. They were softer than he had imagined, and his heart soared when she let out a little moan and kissed him back.

"*Corlan!*" bellowed King Herbert.

The shout was so loud that at first he thought her father was in the room with them. Instantly they jumped apart as he looked around the empty library.

"Corlan, my son! I need you now!" The shout ricocheted off the castle walls.

Glancing at Snow's startled features, Corlan held her hand and they ran from the room.

"Where are you? You are needed at once!" Now Corlan could tell Herbert was in the main hall.

"What do you think is wrong?" Snow asked as their feet flew down the grand staircase.

He could not begin to answer and so therefore remained silent until they came to her father. His mother was already there, holding her husband's arm. Raven stood next to them.

"I am here! What is needed?" he asked as they approached the king.

"I must leave at once—there has been an uprising with the Yandren court. We are to go to arms immediately and meet them on the outskirts before they invade here in the center of Olivian."

"Yes, sir," Corlan replied, his heart pumping. "I will get my things promptly. Expect me to ride within ten minutes."

Herbert walked forward and placed a hand on his shoulder. "No, my boy. I need you here to protect the women."

"What? I am the greatest swordsman you have. You need me on the battlefront."

"Nay. I need you here!"

Had he done something wrong? "Why?" He tried to hide his disappointment and be obedient, but it was extremely difficult. How would he be able to protect the king if he was not fighting with him?

"You are the best in the land, but I love these women with my life, and so I leave my best to protect them. I must, or I shall worry every single night and day I am gone."

Corlan nodded. "Very well."

"I want you to know that I visited with Hibbens two days ago and changed my last will and testament."

Snow gasped.

"I have named you my heir, should anything happen to me and Snow. You are as much a son to me as any other man could be, and so, I naturally leave it all to you."

Overcome, Corlan hugged his new father. "Sir, I thank you. Though, to be perfectly clear, you are not allowed to die."

Herbert chuckled and pulled back. "I have no plans of having my existence ceased at this early stage in my life." He looked at his new queen, and her hand went out for him. Corlan watched as the king pulled his mother close and kissed her. "I will be back before I am missed," he said.

"Then you tell a falsehood, for you are already missed," she exclaimed as she kissed him again.

Their display reminded Corlan of two very sweet lips he had tasted recently, and he looked over at Snow. Her smile at seeing the love of their parents only made him adore her more. There was not a selfish bone in her body. How kind were her thoughts for everyone. She looked over then and blushed when she caught him staring.

King Herbert's last words were for his daughter as he caught her up in a large bear hug. "If need be, show them all how I have taught you to fight like a lion. Remind our enemy that you are more than a pretty face. And Snow?"

"Yes?"

"I love you." He patted her back. "Trust Corlan with your life. He will see that nothing harms you."

CHAPTER TEN

THE HOUSE BECAME QUITE melancholy after King Herbert left. Snow found herself worried ill most days for his safety and prayed for his quick return.

A week after he had gone, Snow and the others were in the game room attempting their hands at whist. She was particularly anxious today because of the rain—it did not allow her a chance to wander outdoors and forget her troubles.

They had all been keeping a careful eye on Melantha. Snow had seen her scowl in her direction more than once that day. And just after tea, she had grabbed Snow's arm and cornered her in the small alcove near the library. "Where are you going? I did not give you permission to walk these halls."

"Forgive me," Snow had said, shocked at the crazed look in her stepmother's eye. "I did not know."

"You think I do not see all that you are doing," she snarled as she loomed closer to Snow. "You think I do not see what you are attempting to do to us all, but know that I am not fooled! I know of your betrayal. I know of your thoughts."

Snow was so stunned and confused. Melantha was so clearly livid with her that she dared not utter a word in protest.

"You will soon pay for all you have done!" And with that, the queen had spun around and made her way back down the stairs.

Snow did not know what she had done to upset the queen, but she hoped to remain as hidden as possible so as not to trigger any more anger and cause the madness to grow even further.

"Your turn, Snow," Terrance said from across the table. "Woolgathering again, I see."

She grinned as she played her trick. "Yes, well, what other choice do I have?"

"You could join us and play the game," Raven teased.

Snow caught Corlan's gaze and held it. He must have been watching her for a while. "What are you thinking about?" she finally asked him. "Am I woolgathering too much for you as well?"

"No." He released a slow breath. "I assume the same thoughts have been plaguing both our minds," he said before leaning forward and playing his trick.

"I am fairly certain it is similar to what has been niggling in *all* of our thoughts." Raven placed a card down.

Snow watched as everyone looked at each other.

"Correct, Snow?" Terrance asked. "At least, that's what has been worrying me, ever since you told us of your encounter with the queen earlier."

"You are worried about me?"

"Yes, we are all concerned over the way Queen Melantha has been treating you. It is clear you are the first victim of the cursed mirror."

"You feel it too?" she asked them.

Corlan nodded his head and put his cards face-down on the table. "How could we not? It is clearly obvious she is angry with you. I do not feel it will be safe to live here much longer."

"What do you mean?" Her heart grew cold. Would she have to leave her home?

Following Corlan's example, Terrance and Raven put their cards facedown as well and pulled their chairs in closer.

"You have been speaking about me, I can tell." Snow set her hand down. "Well, out with it. What do you know that I do not?"

Corlan cleared his throat. "It is the legend. I was reading up on it, as you are aware, and it would seem that when one person becomes the target, jealously forms about them, a dark desire to see the person dead and removed from their sight."

Snow rubbed her lips together as she attempted to process what he was saying. "And so you believe that to save my life, I will need to leave." She looked up at Raven and Terrance. "You all do? There really is no choice?"

Corlan continued, "Snow, this is indeed something that we can't take lightly. I can't allow you to die. And with your father away, there is even less protection for you. I have no idea what must be going through my mother's head and what she finds about you to despise, but whatever the case, this is real."

"Perhaps she was able to break the enchantment on Snow," Terrance said quietly, his eyes meeting hers.

"Oh, good heavens!" Snow gasped. "But she is so very settled. She has my father, and she is so beautiful! Certainly, I am not to be envied."

"What do you mean?" Corlan asked.

Raven leaned toward Snow. "Yes, what is it that Terrance seems to know, but the rest of us do not?"

"Go on and tell them your fears. It is better that they understand everything."

Snow groaned before muttering, "'Tis nothing. I just wonder if perhaps I am under an enchantment—a spell to make people flock to me. And I have been concerned in the past that a woman will be able to break free of the spell and find me revolting because of the attention I receive." She then spoke the last few words, though it felt almost silly saying them aloud to her friends. "And, depending on her envy, she may wish me dead."

Corlan did not blink. He folded his arms but did not seem upset. "So you have thought this for some time, and you did not think to speak to me of your concerns?"

"I felt foolish."

Both Corlan and Raven glanced at Terrance.

"But clearly you feel at ease in sharing now. It is best that you told someone, so it does not matter who." Rubbing his chin, Corlan thought a moment longer. "I could see what you are saying; perhaps you *are* under a spell of some sort. And there is definitely a very real concern here. We have all witnessed my mother's newfound jealousy of you."

"With the mirror feeding her suspicions, how far will she go to fulfill her covetous rage?" Terrance asked.

"Death," Raven whispered. "Just as Snow fears." She turned to Corlan. "You know Mother has always had a darker, passionate side. If that glass is convincing her that Snow is a threat, there is nothing we will be able to do to stop her."

"Right. Then Snow leaves now." Corlan stood up.

"No. I can't—I am not even packed. And where would I stay?"

"I know of a place that would have you—I have already checked, though I do not wish to mention it within these walls. I feel at times they have ears."

"And with their loyalty for their new queen, I do not believe we can trust the servants anymore. It is safer not to say too much," Raven pointed out.

Snow sensed the panic within her nearly double. Never before had she felt so insecure and unsafe. Would her stepmother and trusted servants really turn against her?

Corlan stood, leaning his fists on the table and spoke directly to her. "If you are not willing to leave this moment, at least promise me that you will have a small portmanteau packed with a few of your belongings tonight so we may leave at a moment's notice, if need be."

She nodded. "Very well. I can do that."

"Snow, I will not have you harmed by this mirror in any way. I promised I would protect you. I meant that—you will always be completely safe with me."

"Thank you." She smiled, her heart warmed by his goodness. Honestly, she knew of no man like him, and though he had not kissed her again since before her father left, she had dreamed of it many times. Even then she wished they were alone. *I wonder if he would kiss me now if no one was around.*

"So, who would like to brave the queen in her quarters and ferret out her thoughts of Snow?" Terrance asked.

"No one but me will ever go in those rooms." Corlan sat back down. "I can't risk the mirror seeing of any of you."

"Will you attempt to speak with her?" Raven inquired.

"Aye." Corlan took a deep breath. "I will speak with her tonight once she has had a nice supper."

"Should I attend the meal?" Snow fidgeted in her seat. "Or would you prefer me to be gone?"

"You should come so as not to draw attention to yourself, though I would have you sit away from her."

"You know Mother is particular in her table placements," Raven protested. "She will always have the table situated by rank. Snow must be close to her now that King Herbert is gone. Snow is the next heir."

Corlan threw his hands up. "Women will forever plague me. She will have to accept the fact that Snow will not be sitting next to her and that is that. I will not have Snow poisoned or something worse because of etiquette. Hang convention!"

"I have a solution," Terrance chimed in. "Why do we not have Snow entertain your special guest?" He inclined his head. "I have no problem playing that role for supper."

"Terrance!" Raven beamed. "You are a genius! It is perfect. We shall say you requested to have Snow sit with you. Mother knows you are here to court her—this will not even cause her to blink an eyelid."

"Perfect." Snow smiled genuinely for the first time that day. "Thank you. Let us survive the next few hours and then we will go from there." She stood from the table, leaving her cards upon it.

"I believe I will get an early start on the packing. Just to be safe."

After a glance at Corlan, Raven stood up. "I can help. We will see you boys at supper."

Snow watched Terrance grin as they walked to the door. Then as they were leaving, he said, "Boys? Is this the modern cant they are using? Royal princes are now reduced to mere boys?"

Corlan laughed as they stepped out. "You have not met the strong women of Olivian, have you? There is much more to experience than just feeling like a schoolboy among them."

Raven dipped her head back inside and called, "We only do it because we know you love it so!" before grinning with Snow down the corridor and to her rooms.

CHAPTER ELEVEN

AT THE DINING TABLE, Corlan sat on his mother's right-hand side. He watched her glance many times in Snow's direction. Melantha became more irritated with each smile Snow gave Terrance. By the end of the meal, his mother was positively incensed.

Corlan had tried to keep the conversation light and entertain her, but to no avail. Her thoughts were most maddeningly centered on Snow White.

"Mother, are you well?" he finally asked, hoping the rage he saw within her eyes was perhaps a trick of the candlelight. They were red-rimmed and weary from missing her new husband.

Those eyes snapped to his. "No, I am not well!" she fiercely whispered. "I am through playing these amusing games. I want you in my chambers directly following the dessert tray. I have much to discuss with you, and much more to plan. It is time for you to grow, my son."

"What do you mean?"

"Hush," she hissed. Her eyes took on an eerie bright-green glow for a moment before settling back into their normal grayish-green. "I will speak of all this later." She abruptly stood up. "I will have dessert in my rooms. To be here another moment would make me even more ill than I currently am."

With that, she left the little party in a huff and slammed the door behind her.

"'Tis me, is it not? She loathes me," Snow said in a quiet voice.

Corlan glanced at the servants standing about waiting to attend them and then smiled at Snow. "Of course she does not." His voice held a tinge of warning to be aware of listening ears.

Thankfully, Snow knew him well and took the hint. "Yes, you are probably correct. She is more than likely having a wretched time missing my father and so has been a bit irritable lately. I will not take it personally."

The rest of supper consisted of polite small talk and there was no occasion for Corlan to speak to any of them before he had to leave to see his mother. "Please forgive me; my mother has requested that I meet her in her rooms at this time." He stood up and bowed, giving Snow a look that promised to reveal all later.

As he made his way up to Melantha's quarters, climbing the stairs and traversing through the corridors, he wondered at her cryptic words. What design had the mirror placed within her, and how in the world would he be able to protect Snow from her targeted wrath? He needed to stay one move ahead of her and prayed he would know what she was planning before it occurred. At least for now, his mother trusted him. But how long would that trust last if she knew his real thoughts?

He tapped lightly upon the door.

"Come in, Corlan," she called. When he entered, she smiled at her reflection and said, "I knew it was you. The mirror told me."

"Really?" Corlan fought for control of his emotions. The looking glass was clearly becoming too powerful.

"Yes. He said the next person who knocked upon my door would be my son. And he was correct. He tells me everything." She moved away from the glass and sat upon her bed, her yellow silk skirts fanning prettily around her. She seemed much happier now.

"What else has he been telling you?" Corlan asked cautiously as he walked toward the bench at the foot of her bed.

She grinned and fell back into her luxurious pillows, her glorious hair forming a halo of fire around her head. Then she giggled a bit before saying, "He is simply the most wonderful being who ever was. After conversing with him just now, I know exactly what must be done with Snow White." She sighed. "It is like he takes all these horrid trials from my life and lifts the heavy burdens right off my shoulders. He is the friend I never knew I needed."

"Indeed!" Corlan rested a foot upon the bench. "And what have you two been planning for Snow?"

"That is where you come in. It is the most perfect solution—I do not know how I did not see it for myself." She giggled again.

"You would have *me* do something?" It was difficult to remain calm when every word she spoke made him angrier.

"Yes. It is brilliant, and will solve all our problems involving Snow."

He brought his hand up to inspect his nails nonchalantly. "What exactly are these crimes you have to lay at her feet?"

"What?" Melantha sat up. "Are you jesting? You truly have no idea why I find the girl so revolting?"

He met her gaze. "None."

All at once she was raving. "Then let me explain! First," she began as she climbed off the bed and walked over to him, "your sister will have no chance at finding a man while that harpy continues to steal all of her suitors away! I had great hopes for her and Prince Terrance. Great hopes! Finally, it would seem that a man noticed our dearest Raven! But no!" She spun on her heel and began to pace. "No, he is as smitten with Snow as the rest of them are! It is greatly frustrating to see your sister's pretty face being overlooked because of Snow's confounded beauty! I wish I could scratch the girl's eyes out, she infuriates me so!"

"Mother, you do not—"

"Do not speak to me!" she interrupted. "The mirror has told me of Snow's amusement and hatred of poor Raven. Snow has always planned to ruin any chance of happiness your sister has, and I will not stand by and watch it happen. I will guarantee that girl never harms your sister again!"

She walked over to the large window and drew back the curtain, showing the darkened sky.

Clearly she was not willing to hear any opinion except that of the mirror, so Corlan waited until he was certain she was done speaking before he asked, "What do you plan to do with Snow?"

She smirked and turned from the window. "Not me. *You.* You shall do it."

"I shall do what?"

Slowly she walked toward him, her features taking on a happy, youthful glee. "It will be the perfect revenge, having you do it. And everything will sort itself out so wonderfully. I can't wait!"

Corlan's hands began to shake slightly, the trepidation he felt enhanced as he choked out, "Again, I ask you, what? What have you and that mirror planned for me to do to Snow White?"

She blinked and then chuckled. "Why, to kill her."

"What?" He was going to be ill. "You wish *me* to kill Snow?"

"Of course! Who better to handle a sword?" She clutched his lapels. "I want her heart, Corlan!" Her face contorted as she whispered, "You will take her away and then cut out her heart! I shall eat it. The mirror has promised me that if I eat Snow White's heart, I shall acquire her loveliness and be beautiful forever!"

"You are mad!" he shouted as he pushed against her.

Surprisingly, her strength exceeded his as she clung on. "No, my dear boy, it is not madness—it is anger I feel. And once Snow is gone, you shall be the heir to both our kingdoms, and Raven shall marry her prince. Do you not see how faultless this plan is?"

"No!" Corlan tried again to pull away, the fear in his heart far overshadowing his earlier fury. He had to get Snow out of here. He had to keep her away from his mother at all costs, and they needed to leave immediately.

"No?" She yanked him toward her. "Is my son daring to disobey me?"

"I—"

"Mirror!" she shouted as trails of green smoke began to pour from the glass. "Force him! Force him to do as we say! He will kill her. He will bring back her heart. He will have no choice!"

"Never!" Corlan shoved against his mother. Bringing one foot to her waist, he pushed her away from him and darted for the door as the green mist started to lap against his shoes. It was quick, much faster than before. He felt it rising and encompassing his legs, torso, arms, hands. He rushed to the door and yanked upon it to the sound of his mother laughing. It was locked. It would not budge. As he struggled with the door, the green mist enveloped him whole.

CHAPTER TWELVE

AFTER SUPPER, SNOW EXCUSED herself from Raven and Terrance.

"You do not want to stay and have tea with us in the parlor?" Raven asked.

"No, I would rather hear directly from Corlan. I think I will wait for him in my rooms."

Terrance grinned. "What, and leave us out of the gossip? 'Tis not fair."

Snow smiled. "Yes, but I promise to tell you everything later."

That had been over a quarter of an hour ago. What could be taking him so long? Wringing her hands, she walked from the window to the door and then back to the window again. Nothing seemed to sit well with her. If things were as bad as everyone seemed to think they were, she would more than likely be leaving in the morning. Glancing at her packed portmanteau, she wondered for the tenth time if she was perhaps forgetting something of importance.

Finally, there was a knock at her door.

He is here! "Yes?" she called out.

"Let me in," Corlan replied.

She rushed to the door and opened it. "So, is it as bad as we think?"

"Come with me now. We must leave the castle," he commanded, his voice gruffer than usual as he entered the room.

Goodness, already? "Right now?" Butterflies exploded within her stomach.

"Yes, we must leave at once."

His gaze skimmed over her, not meeting her eyes as he searched her room. She could tell he was thinking of all that had transpired with Melantha. "But it is dark," she hedged, and then, not able to resist, she asked, "What happened?"

Ignoring the question, Corlan walked over to the wardrobe and fetched her cloak. "Put this on," he said as he handed it to her and then picked up her bag which she'd set next to it. "Hurry. We do not have time to dally."

"Corlan?" Her heart began to race. "Corlan, what are you hiding from me? Why will you not say what happened? You are behaving so oddly."

He halted at the door and turned toward her. "There is no time to explain. We are leaving this instant. Now come!"

"Will I have a moment to say good-bye to Raven?"

"Certainly not," he said as he stepped into the hallway and then whispered, "Now, complete silence until we leave the castle."

Whatever Melantha had said to him must have been awful. Snow scurried to follow him out of the bedroom and down the narrow servants' stairs and out the back entrance of the palace.

"We are to head to the forest as quickly as possible," he commanded. His pace across the damp grass of the darkened castle lawn was brisk and it was hard for her to keep up. Looking back at her, he yelled, "Run!" with such fierceness it startled her into a frantic sprint.

As she came up to him, he shouted, "Go!" and pointed with his hand for her to be in front.

What was he protecting her from? She was afraid to look back as she held her skirts and passed him, beginning to run as fast as she could toward the dark forest.

"Keep moving!"

She could hear his footsteps close behind her.

"Do not turn around, whatever you do!"

Her heart pounded wildly and yet she found the strength to continue on. What was happening? It was as if great beasts were after them. It was all she could imagine, a terrible monster of some sort chasing them into the woods. She was running too fast to be able to speak or even breathe properly. All she could think was to hurry, hurry, hurry.

As they reached the forest, she darted into it, dodging shrubbery and rocks and fallen logs.

"Go!" he shouted again when she began to slow her pace.

She pressed onward. The branches snagged and ripped into her cloak, scratching her arms and face and whipping into her legs. And still deeper into the forest they went.

It felt as if they had been running for hours, but it most likely had been less than one. Just when she thought her heart would surely burst, Corlan grabbed her arm and brought her to a halt.

"Stop." His breath came in huge gasps. "We are safe, but do not turn around. I need you to remain perfectly still."

They had come to a small clearing. The moon lit the meadow from behind them and even in her fright she loved how pretty it looked in the darkened sky. Heaving in breaths, she held perfectly still as he commanded and tried to focus on the meadow and not how hard her heart was beating within her chest.

Corlan's shadow loomed to her right. She smiled when she thought of how protective he was. He was so strong and wonderful to guard her—she did not feel half as scared knowing he was there.

His shadow moved and she saw that he unsheathed a dagger from his hip.

Was there danger? She took a deep breath and willed herself not to panic. *Remain perfectly still*, he had said. There must be some threat nearby. But no matter what was out in these woods, she knew he would defend her with his life. His skill with the blade was beyond anything she had ever known.

"Hold very still," she heard him whisper.

Watching his shadow on the ground, she saw him raise the dagger above his head. His arms began to tremble above her. And then she heard a loud groan. Was he hurting? It did not make sense. His arms were above him, not battling something.

Did he need help? When she heard him groan again, she turned just as his hands dropped and the dagger plunged at her.

CHAPTER THIRTEEN

CORLAN SAW THE SHOCKED look upon Snow's face as she crouched instinctively to get away, and it woke a greater part of him. At the last second, he yanked the dagger to the left and sliced her sleeve rather than plunging it into her chest, leaving a long scratch upon her arm. He felt that if he did not murder Snow, he would cease to exist, so strong had been the urge forged within his heart.

Though the need to slay her raged inside him, his love for her fought against it. The fierce battle within him to hold the knife steady took every ounce of strength and control he had. He could not fling it aside—the thing would not leave his hands.

"Argh!" His hands flew upward again. "No!" He plunged the knife again and forced it away once more, missing her by mere millimeters. Instantly, his arms jerked upward, ready to repeat the process again and again.

"Go!" he shouted to Snow. He planted his feet into the ground and fought to keep the dagger as far away as possible from her.

She stood up. "What are you doing?" He had never seen her so frightened before as she stared in horror at his shaking arms. "Corlan, stop! Please stop!"

It hurt to breathe, let alone speak when all of his energy was used to combat the mirror's spell. Clenching his jaw, he attempted to convey what was happening even as his body protested. "You . . . have to run . . . now."

"Corlan? What is it?" She stepped several paces back.

It took every ounce of his might to stop the dagger. He could only battle his quivering legs a few seconds before they began to follow her.

She scrambled backward faster. "Corlan, is it the mirror? Did your mother do something to you?"

"Yes!" he grunted as he tried to halt his feet from chasing her. "I…have to… kill you. Run, Snow! Go!"

She choked on a sob. "Corlan, no! I can't leave without you! Please, stop." Unable to see where she was going, she stumbled over a rock and fell to the ground.

Instantly, he sprinted the last few feet to her, his large body looming over above hers.

"No!" she cried as she covered her face with her hands.

He howled as his arms lunged downward. At the last second, he yanked the dagger away again and growled as it sank into his own thigh.

He toppled over in agony as Snow scrambled to her feet and stepped toward him. "Oh, no!" she whispered.

"Get out of here! Leave, before I kill you!" he shouted.

She darted away, but called to him, "I can't leave you like this. You are hurt."

"Snow, now! I am holding the spell at bay with every ounce of strength I have left. When I begin to weaken, you will die if you are anywhere in my vicinity."

Her breathing came in frightful gasps. She sounded so lost and alone. "Where do I go?"

"I can't say. You will have to find your own place. Anything I say to you at this time gives power to the mirror and Melantha to find you. Now, go!" Flipping over onto his back, his hands wrenched the knife from his leg and he saw with satisfaction that Snow gathered up her skirts and ran with all her might, fleeing into the forest.

He closed his eyes, hoping that if he did not see where she went, he would not be able to follow. Even that was a struggle, keeping his eyes closed.

He began to feel the edge of the spell wearing off the further away she went. It was fascinating to feel the urgency to murder her rushing through his veins. He could almost taste her fear. He wanted it, needed it, but it was not so powerful as before.

What had become of him? He wanted to weep. He wanted to curl into a ball and sob. What had he done to her? His sweet, sweet Snow. Now she was terrified of him.

Now she would never wish to be around him again.

She *could* never be around him again.

All was lost. It was hopeless.

Corlan lay upon the ground, his eyes still closed, for several more minutes. He could not risk finding her.

After the despair sank in, he began to become angry at his mother. How could she have done this to him? How could any of this be what she truly desired? The foolish woman had ruined everything—simply everything he had ever dreamed of having. Snow could never come home again. He would never have a chance at her hand now!

His mother was a stupid, selfish hag!

Irritated, he sat up. The action caused fresh blood to pour from his wound. He grimaced as he took off his shirt and wrapped it around his thigh. At least the knife had landed in him and not her, forcing his body to halt its chase. It ended up being the perfect way to allow her to escape. Slowly he climbed to his feet and began the long walk back toward the castle, limping as he went. He stopped and gathered his bag and Snow's luggage before proceeding forward.

His small pack held a beautifully carved box the queen had given him.

He needed a heart for his mother to eat so she could believe it was Snow's beauty filling her.

Melantha deserved no beauty!

Someone whose soul had become so ugly warranted something just as hideous.

Corlan grinned as he limped. He knew just the place to go—King Herbert's personal farm.

My, my, my… What a surprise his mother would have when he finally announced that she had eaten the heart of a pig.

CHAPTER FOURTEEN

SNOW RAN WITH ALL her might through the darkened forest, dodging trees and shrubs and fallen logs and all sorts of hazardous rocks and dips in the ground. She ran and ran and ran until she simply could not run anymore. And then she walked. When her walking eventually slowed to a stop, she collapsed against a large pine tree and wrapped her ripped cloak about her.

She was lost.

Alone.

And so very afraid.

It was not right that princesses should cry and so she attempted bravely not to do so. But the memory of Corlan lunging at her with that knife caused her to shut her eyes tight. He was going to kill her. He was commanded to kill her.

This was beyond her worst fears.

Why Corlan? Of all people, why him?

Burying her face in her hands, she slipped to the forest floor that was covered in pine needles and leaves and she sobbed until she could not cry another moment. And then with tear-filled gasps she eventually fell asleep, too exhausted to care if Corlan found her or not. Her last thoughts were of her father, somewhere very far away battling to save them all.

"Father, I love you," she whispered as she drifted to sleep. "Prevail and come home soon. I need you. We all need you."

***

"DID YOU DO AS I asked?" Melantha demanded when Corlan came into her chambers later that night. She wore her robe and slippers, but it looked as though she had not slept, probably anxious for him to return.

"I have the heart for you in here," he replied in a monotone voice. He passed the ornate box over to her as she lounged upon the red velvet sofa near her window.

He saw her looking over his bloodstained torso and leg.

Glancing down, he blinked, surprised to see the amount of gore the pig had left on him. Cutting out a heart was a messy business. He had deposited the dead animal in the chef's butchery room to be found the next morning.

"Really, Corlan, you need to clean yourself up and get dressed. It is improper to be walking around like that. What if someone were to see you?"

Did she honestly think he would care at this point? "What is wrong, Mother?" he asked. "Are you worried about what others might think? Truly? Is this your greatest concern right now?" He walked backward a few steps and bowed low, mocking her. "Knowing that your stepdaughter is dead does not trigger anything within you, only how your son will be portrayed without his shirt on, covered in blood?" Straightening, he continued, "Did you not think this was how I would appear after your gruesome task was performed? How should I have approached you, then—bathed and freshly dressed?"

"Corlan, enough!" She stood up, clutching the box to her chest. "Your sarcasm is not acceptable. We are protecting our family, our kingdom. Snow White was the biggest threat to us. Now that she is gone, we can finally go forward with our plans for peace."

Hardened and numb against anything the woman said, Corlan did not even attempt to disagree. There was no shock left within him at her words and actions. She had removed all the good left inside.

He was simply hollow now, a mere shell of the man he once was.

She giggled as she lifted the lid of the box and asked, "Would you like to see what becomes of me? You will be astounded! The mirror has promised that it will be extraordinary!"

He smirked. "You will eat it now? Raw?"

Glancing up in surprise, she said, "Of course! I must. But it will be worth it to receive all the beauty I deserve now that she is gone."

He grimaced. Perhaps he was not as immune to her plans as he believed. This woman before him was certainly no longer the mother who had raised him.

She walked to the looking glass and chanted while the green mist began to fill the room.

"Mirror, mirror on the wall,
Beseeching thine assistance, I do call
As this heart within the box
Speaks of a fairer beauty that mocks.
I ask you grant *me* the beauty fair

To wind itself through me its splendor share

Partaking of its glories be

Give me the power to become like she."

Again, Corlan could not move his body while she spoke, nor he could hear the reply of the mirror. Disgusted, he closed his eyes as Melantha reached in the box and began to eat the heart. The sloshing, wet sounds of her eating nearly made him ill.

He knew she was finished when he heard her snickering. Opening his eyes, he saw her full of glee, wiping the red blood from her face with a cloth that had been upon her dresser. "I am ready!" she shouted to her ceiling. "I am ready to become the fairest in the land."

The green smoke wrapped itself around her ankles and then slowly spun up her body and over her head. Melantha continued to chortle with excitement. When her laughter turned to cackles, the smoke began to fade away. Corlan stared in fascinated horror at the hideous woman before him. Short, gray wisps of hair barely covered her balding, aged-spotted scalp. Her back was bent and twisted, her face a series of deep lines and hideous warts. She looked old enough to knock upon her grave.

His limbs began to release as the smoke faded away and his mother ran for the mirror. Corlan flinched, ready for her screams, but was surprised when her glee continued. Could she not see herself? He stepped over to view her reflection and let out a stunned breath when he saw the beautiful woman in the glass.

Indeed, Melantha had no idea how truly hideous she had become. She could only see what she wished for more than anything.

A striking woman in her late teens, with fiery hair and smooth skin, stared back at her.

The enchanted mirror showed lies to feed her vanity.

No matter the cost, she could never know what she actually looked like. As quickly as possible, he removed himself from her chambers. Melantha was so enthralled with the beauty in the looking glass that she did not even glance over when he shut the door.

He limped as quickly as he could to the guest wing and into Terrance's rooms. Thank goodness the castle was asleep or talk of his bloodied, naked chest would be gossip throughout the village. As it was, he woke only the sleeping prince.

"Terrance! Terrance!" he shouted as he entered. "I need help immediately!"

CHAPTER FIFTEEN

"ARE YOU OUT OF your wits?" asked Terrance as Corlan explained everything. "You want to remove all the castle mirrors within the next couple of hours?"

"Yes! And we must hurry. Get dressed, man!" Corlan said.

Terrance rubbed his face and then chuckled. "My nightclothes are a sight more decent than you are, chap. Perhaps *you* need to get dressed."

Corlan looked down and laughed. "Touché." Hobbling toward the door, he said, "I will be back quickly. Meet me in the library and I will see about waking Raven to help as well."

"Raven?" Terrance grinned. "In that case, you win. I will meet you there in about five minutes."

"Ha! I see how it is. You will come if a maiden is present."

"Corlan, one day you will come to understand—it is always about the maidens being present. There is something about them that allows a man to become his best self."

Corlan shook his head and shut the door.

Terrance got out of bed and let out a whistle of amazement, a bit stunned as he dressed. Snow was gone, left alone in some forest. Corlan had no chance of saving her or protecting her at all. And the witch had become an old hag after eating the heart of a pig. He smirked, enjoying the irony, and then scolded himself for smiling.

He always did find humor at the most inappropriate times. If he did not learn to control that peculiar habit, one day it would be sure to get him into trouble.

Sighing a bit, he pulled on his boots and allowed the heaviness of the situation to hit him as he stomped his feet to fit more comfortably. What a mess they were all in. Hopefully Snow would find a place to remain hidden until they resolved the queen's betrayal. He worried about her though, and he could tell Corlan was beside himself with fear for her safety. Though neither of them mentioned it, Terrance knew they were both worried about wolves or other beasts.

Taking an oil lamp, he slipped out of his room and made his way down the darkened corridors to the library. Perhaps there was a chance he could go find Snow himself and guarantee that she was safe. Excitement poured through his limbs at the thought. Yes! It was the perfect solution. Allow *him* to protect her.

He waited until Corlan came back to suggest the idea to him.

So eager was he to share the news that he did not see Raven slip in until she said, "So, now you, rather than Corlan, will become Snow's hero?"

Terrance glanced over and smiled, his heart jolting at the sight of her. She looked stunning, her long hair shimmering in the soft glow of the lamps around them. "Hello." When she did not reply and appeared to be waiting, he thought back on the question she had asked. "Yes. Yes, it will be me who claims the hero part, I imagine. Though,"—he turned to Corlan—"did you not tell her what happened?"

"Corlan explained the spell on the way to the library." Raven seemed upset as she fidgeted a bit.

"What is wrong?" Terrance asked.

The look she gave him would have soured milk. "Honestly?" she snapped. "You must inquire if something is wrong?"

"I—uh…"

She flipped her long braid over her shoulder. "My sister is alone in a forest, running for her life. My mother has become so darkened by a cursed mirror that she has eaten a pig's heart, believing it to be Snow's, and has turned herself into an old woman." She threw her hands up and crossed to a tall window. Pointing outside, she continued, "My stepfather is battling for his life and may very well be the first person in this family to die, though the others do not fare much better." Turning around, she looked at Corlan. "And my dear brother, the one who was left to protect me and Snow, has now been enchanted by the mirror as well and has to overcome every bit of personal battle training he has had *not* to hunt and kill my best friend!"

She walked up to Terrance, her eyes snapping fire. "It is nearly four in the morning. I have not slept well and I awaken to hear we must remove all the mirrors in the castle immediately. And then I come in here to see you eager to leave me and become the true hero of

Snow's story." She pushed against his chest. "And you have the gall to ask what is wrong. Honestly? Am I to lose *everything* tonight?"

He quickly captured her hands before she pushed him again. "Raven, enough."

She tugged against his hold. "Let go of me!"

"No. I will not. Not until you allow your thoughts to calm down." He tugged on her wrists and brought her in close. "Come here." He slowly wrapped an arm around her, his other hand still holding both of hers, and then whispered, "I beg your pardon. Forgive me." When he felt her melt a bit in his arms, he gently released her hands and tucked her fully into his embrace.

"I loathe you," Raven mumbled into his chest.

"No, you do not."

"Yes, I do." She sniffled and then the sobs came. "I have never despised anyone more in my life."

"Shh…" He pressed a kiss upon the top of her head and felt her arms go around his middle.

"I wish you had never come. Ever." She sobbed harder.

"Why is that?" he asked softly as he left a kiss on her brow.

"Because then I would not be crying right now."

"Nay. You would still be crying."

"I would?"

"Yes, you would. Especially with all the circumstances you are facing. But it is easier to blame me, is it not?"

Her shoulders began to shake.

"Raven," he whispered, his hands trailing upon her back. "Hush. It is all well. You are welcome to shed tears upon any part of my shirt you wish."

"I want to detest you. Why can I not detest you? It would be so much easier for me if you would stop being wonderful, so halt this nonsense now." She pulled back and dashed at her tears. Her gaze would not meet his. "Tell me the truth. Tell me how she has won your heart like all the other hearts she has claimed so I can go back to what I know is best. Tell me you are smitten with my sister. " She stepped away from him. "I was up all night, dreading sleep, because I know that one of these days I will wake up and it will happen. So let us get ourselves over this misery now and allow me to wish you both my felicitations and exceeding hap—happiness." Her shoulders began to shake again.

"Oh, my word." Corlan laughed. "And woman say men are the lesser sex. Have they not a brain in those heads of theirs?"

Raven opened her mouth to say something, but Terrance interceded. "No. She has had enough wrestling with her fears at this time. You will not be goading her on." He nodded toward the door. "Go start removing the mirrors—we will join you shortly."

Corlan stared at him a moment. "Are you ordering me about in the castle that very well could be mine one day?"

"Just so. Now get, you!" He waved his hand and glanced at Raven. "I have some things I wish to say to your sister, and I do not need prying ears around."

Corlan took a deep breath. "Be quick about it. We simply can't stop every time one of these women begins to act like—well, a woman."

"Again, one day you will truly understand that it is always about the women."

CHAPTER SIXTEEN

ONCE CORLAN LEFT, RAVEN took a deep breath and glanced at Terrance.

He grinned ruefully and held out a hand. "Do you still despise me?"

She looked at that hand and bit her lip, worrying it. Should she trust him? His gaze met hers and she saw such gentleness in his eyes, tugging at her from within their depths. Cautiously she stepped forward and placed her hand in his.

He walked them to the settee near the largest of the bookshelves and sat down with her. "May I say something?" he asked as their fingers interlocked.

Why did she dread this conversation so much? Why did she have such anticipation for it? It thrilled her, yet terrified her at the same time. "Yes."

"I have spoken to Snow about you. We were very frank with each other, and she was more than eager to step aside to allow you and me time to decide if we could possibly get along with each other." He brought her knuckles up and kissed them. "Since then, I have observed the way she watches Corlan and the manner in which he can't help but gaze at her. They are very much in love."

"Oh." Raven met his eyes. "So, now you are turning toward me?"

He chuckled. "It is simply baffling the way your treacherous mind creates these situations within it." Leaning near her, he said, "Raven, I was turned toward you before I met Snow. And though I feel a pull for her, it is not nearly as much as the interest I feel in you."

Her heart seemed to stop altogether. "What exactly are you saying?"

"I am saying, my dear, that I would like very much to continue as we are. I would like you not to worry about my intentions toward anyone other than you, for I have none for any woman but you."

"Truly?" She could not believe her ears. Was there not another princess who had captured him?

"Yes. I would ask that you learn to trust me. I will not harm you." His eyes trailed over her features. "I know it has been a hard road for you until now, so it shall take some time to see that I am really all that I profess to be. And that is fine—I need time as well."

Time was probably a very good thing. "I can understand that."

"I would like to get to know you more—what I have already found has enticed me greatly. But I want to guarantee that this could work for both of us. I am not here to select a wife—I came to Olivian to find a partner, someone equally willing to love me as well. I do not believe in these old-fashioned practices where men come and bargain for the women they fancy. Nay, the girl I marry will come to me freely because she wishes it as greatly as I do. Because we are equal partners first—in love, in station, in life."

"Thank you," Raven whispered. She had never felt her heart so warmed before.

"I see you are amazed at what I have said." He tugged her hand. "I will wait until you trust these words, until we are both willing to go further."

Not sure what else to do, but completely overwhelmed by his goodness and patience, Raven leaned forward and surprised herself by kissing him in reply.

***

WHEN SNOW AWOKE THE next day, it was nearly mid-afternoon. She felt the faint warm breeze caress her cheek as her eyes fluttered open to the brightness. Slowly she was brought back to reality as she observed the foliage around her. The birds chirped merrily above her head as the leaves rustled with the breeze, making it sound as if she were near a river. Snow turned upon her back, looking up at those tall branches above her and then squinting as the sun peeked through them while they swayed.

This was not such a bad place. It seemed peaceful and completely the opposite from the horrors it appeared to be in the dark. She stretched and felt her taut muscles protest. She had never run so fast and so far in all her life and her body most certainly felt the brunt of her escapades from the night before.

Goodness, she was so stiff.

Her stomach growled. Apparently her limbs were not the only thing protesting—she was famished. But to lie here a moment longer would feel so wonderful. She stretched again.

She contemplated rising and finding some summer berries to eat when suddenly a bright spark popped before her eyes.

She blinked and then sat up as it darted away.

What was that?

Scanning the area, she found the spark of light again, this time about ten feet from her in a bush. It quickly dashed away and then reappeared right in front of her. Startled, she fell back on her elbows and watched, fascinated, as the little twinkling light came toward her. It flitted around her face for a few moments before zooming upwards, where it flickered high on a branch above her.

"Hello?" Snow called up to it. "What are you?"

Just then another spark of light caught her attention in a shrubbery about five feet in front of her. She sat up and had brought her knees in to stand up when that light began to sparkle and bounce toward her.

She froze.

Its luminosity increased into a much larger spark than the other one.

Entranced, Snow smiled as the light came all the way up to her, growing in size until it was about a foot tall and then resting upon her knee.

"Hello?" she asked again as she noticed yet another bright spark pop to life a few feet on her right. And then another and another.

Slowly, the one before her dimmed and Snow caught her breath when a tiny ethereal woman in a flowing pink gown stood before her. She had beautiful lavender slanted eyes with long lashes, a thin nose, and a small pink mouth. Her lavender ponytail caught the breeze and flowed around her shoulders briefly before settling behind her back again.

Snow was amazed that she could not even feel the weight of the woman's dainty feet upon her knee, and then she understood why. The lovely being unfolded the most alluring gossamer wings upon either side of her shoulders. They fluttered and glittered in the sunlight, their iridescent colors changing from yellow to pink and then back again.

"You are a fairy!"

CHAPTER SEVENTEEN

THE FAIRY GRINNED AND bowed her head. "Yes, I am. And you are the fairest Snow White."

"How do you know who I am?" Snow asked, not taking her eyes off the pretty creature. Never before had she dreamed of meeting a fairy up close.

"We have always known who you are, which is why we have been searching all night for you."

"We?"

"Yes, my sisters and I."

Snow watched each flash of light transform into a beautiful fairy as they fluttered toward her. There were four! She was actually seeing *four fairies*. Smiling, she felt like a little girl all over again.

The one upon her knee flew up and took her place with the others in a small semicircle above her. "How grateful we are to see you well and alive," she said.

"Did you know I was in trouble?"

"Yes." She smiled. "We know more about you than you realize."

Snow quickly got to her feet to see the fairies better. Each one had hair the same color as their eyes. One had beautiful turquoise-colored hair, one blue, and the other green. Their shimmering wings matched their different-colored gowns as well. Snow had so many questions, but first things first. "What are your names?"

The lavender-haired fairy said, "I am Sunday Grace, but you are welcome to call me anything you would like."

"Hello, Grace." Snow curtsied before her, charmed by her name.

"This is Tuesday Hope," said the fairy as she pointed to the turquoise-haired girl. "The blue one is Thursday Peace, and green is Saturday Brave." The mystical women bowed their heads and smiled.

"There are three days missing. Does that mean there are more fairies?"

Grace laughed, her voice sounding like tinkling bells. "Of course. But I will introduce you to them when we bring you to our home."

"Your home?"

"Well, my dear, we could not leave you here to be eaten by wolves, now could we? No, we promised Queen Lilith years ago that we would care for you and guarantee that nothing harmed you."

"You knew my mother?" All at once Snow felt like she was going to cry. Here was a connection she had been wishing to find, someone who had known her mother well and could possibly share more about her than her father ever did.

"Yes, we have assured your protection all this time. Queen Lilith saved me from a woodman's trap, and in return, as a thank you, we have seen to your success and safety."

Snow's jaw dropped. "I *have* been under an enchantment! You placed one upon me, did you not? To make sure everyone I meet loves me."

The fairies glanced at each other. "Yes, it was us. That was one way we could guarantee your security. We knew if you were enchanted, no one would harm you."

Peace pushed a lock of her blue hair off her shoulder. "But we felt the energy in your spell waver yesterday, and we knew someone had been able to break through our magic charm and complete their own dark curse to destroy you. We have been searching high and low ever since."

"I do not think you will ever understand how happy we are to have finally found you." Hope fluttered faster.

"Yes," said Brave. "There was a time last night when the tension was so strong, we feared you would be gone before we could find you."

"I nearly was. But Prince Corlan was able to withstand the curse long enough for me to escape."

"The prince! He has been the one to break our enchantment?" Brave placed her hands on her hips. "If that man is seeking to destroy you, we shall kill him first!"

Great heavens! "No! It was his mother, Queen Melantha, and her wedding gift, the Lythereon Mirror, who have broken the spell."

The fairies gasped, but Snow rushed on. "Corlan is their pawn. My stepmother placed a curse upon him to murder me. He withstood as long as possible, even stabbing himself in the leg to allow me escape. Please do not harm him. Please, I can't lose him."

"My dearie!" Hope exclaimed as she flitted toward her. "We promise not to damage him. But this can't be a good thing at all, using the Lythereon Mirror against you."

"We must get her inside immediately. Who knows what the looking glass has seen already!" Peace rushed forward and pulled on Snow's tattered cape. "Quickly, let us get her out of this forest. There are too many eyes and ears around to be fully comfortable."

"'Tis true," said Grace. "You can't be certain you are alone while in the forest. Goodness! You should have said earlier it was the mirror after you." She held on to another portion of Snow's cape. "Hope and Brave, come and hold her front and back so we may be able to get her home as quickly as possible."

The two fairies fluttered over. One pulled upon the front of her skirts and the other tugged upon the back of her cape. Now she had fairies on all four sides of her, tugging on her clothing. How would this help? They looked as though they would have Snow walk in different directions.

"Now!" Brave said just before Snow saw the forest disappear.

When she felt her stomach drop as though she was falling, she flinched and closed her eyes. A moment later, she opened them and found to her astonishment she was in a parlor of a cozy cottage. There was a bright sunshine streaming through the windows and lacy white curtains. And the aroma of apple pie and homemade bread wafting through the rooms. "Where am I? It smells delicious!"

Hope giggled. "I would say the little one is hungry."

"She must be, or the first thing that would have popped out of her mouth after traveling fairyflight would have been, 'Unbelievable! Can we do it again?'" Grace said.

Snow walked into the red-and-white kitchen. "Forgive me. Yes, it was astonishing to fly like that, and very convenient." She found the pies sitting in the window. Not wanting to appear rude, she said, "But do not worry yourselves over my hunger. I am perfectly fine." She turned around and was startled to see that the fairies were now as tall as she, their wings tucked away. "Oh!"

They all chuckled and pressed forward.

"Come sit down," said Hope. "By the way your gaze was devouring the pies, you are clearly famished." She pointed to a clean table with a floral tablecloth.

"You are full-size now." Snow sat upon the polished wooden chair. "Is this how you usually look?"

Grace turned to Brave, ignoring the question. "Will you use the horn so the others will know we have found Snow White and they may return home?"

"Yes."

Snow watched Brave leave out the side door. A few seconds later, she returned.

"Thank you," said Grace. Then seeing Snow's confusion, she added, "It is not a sound humans can hear." She placed a loaf of bread upon the table. A small wisp of steam floated from it. It smelled wonderful.

"And as for our size, this is not the easiest way for us to appear, but we felt it would be best for you if we did so. The whole cottage has grown significantly to accommodate you."

"Oh." Snow blinked and tried to imagine it much smaller.

When Hope placed a bubbling pot of stew upon the table, Snow's mouth began to water and her stomach rumbled. "How did you make this so quickly?" she asked. "I didn't notice any stew on the stove a moment ago. Did someone stay behind to cook?"

Peace reached over and placed a crock of butter upon the table. "We are magic, dear. Our food always stays perfectly warm until we are ready to eat it."

Just then, three more fairies poofed into the home. The already busy place bustled to life right before her eyes.

"Snow!" they cried, all of them wanting hugs and asking about her adventure and the like. However, Grace put a halt to their queries.

"Enough! She has not eaten, and she is hungry. We will have her answer all our questions once she is full and can divert us properly in the parlor. For now, please sit down and allow the poor girl to eat."

Snow grinned as she looked around the active room. This cottage was so full of energy and colors and happiness. Thank goodness the fairies had found her.

As they bustled around the small dining room and kitchen, chattering and bringing plates and utensils, Snow knew she would love them forever. Who would not want to stay in a magical home with seven sweet fairies?

CHAPTER EIGHTEEN

RAVEN POURED THE TEA while Corlan sat forward in the overstuffed chair in the drawing room. They had managed to remove all the mirrors and place them up in the attic. As long as her mother did not look too closely at her hands—which, thankfully, had not aged as horridly as the rest of her—they might be able to succeed in diverting Melantha from the truth of her looks for a few days longer. Exhausted, they had taken a short break to decide what to do next. Snow was their greatest concern, of course.

"I believe you may be right, Terrance. If we split up, we might have a better chance at succeeding," Corlan said.

"Someone must let King Herbert know what is happening here," Raven said. "Is it wrong to wish to betray your mother like this?"

"No." Terrance shook his head. "If she were the mother you knew, this would not have happened. You can't think of her as your mother again."

"It is true. Unless she can free herself and manage to break the mirror on her own, all will be lost," Corlan said.

Raven pressed her lips together as she placed the tea things on the end table near the settee where she sat. "You are both certain Melantha will die?"

"Yes." Corlan nodded.

When she looked at Terrance, he paused a moment before nodding too.

"Very well, then—we must tell King Herbert. He needs to know what she has done to Snow."

"I would go, but I am afraid to leave Mother right now," Corlan said.

"If I am going to find Snow, that leaves Raven to fetch King Herbert, and there is no way in all of Hades I would allow her to travel to the battlefront."

"I beg your pardon?" Raven sat back in her seat and folded her arms. "If I wish to go and warn King Herbert, there is nothing that would stop me from achieving that. Even you."

Corlan groaned. "Raven, honestly. Let the man protect you."

"I have no problem at all with him protecting me. But when he dictates as he did just now, I feel a little bit testy."

"Testy?" Terrance laughed. "I do find you remarkably refreshing. However, I shall put my foot down again and say, over my lifeless body will you go to King Herbert, *even* if you wished it."

Raven tapped her boot. "Prince Terrance of the Sybright court, need I remind you, as a guest here, that your manners may come off a bit rudely?" She smiled a tight smile, her foot tapping faster.

"Princess Raven of Olivian, no, you do not need to remind me of anything." He stood up and walked toward her. "I am not like most princes who come to woo your sister. Indeed, I am a prince made of much sterner stuff and have actually accepted the challenge of attempting the impossible in wooing *you*. Therefore, if you believe I can't handle a mere stubborn girl who wishes to get herself killed, you must think again."

Raven's heart fluttered wildly while her irritation at his words drove her mind to frenzy. How dare the man speak to her in such a way? How dare he try to rule her? "What of equality and partnership?" She stood up as well. "Or were you merely saying words that would appease me?"

Terrance searched her features. She was not certain what he saw there, but he bowed his head. "Forgive me, Princess. I seem to have been put in my place. By all means, if you wish to go to your stepfather during war, I will not be the man to stand in your way."

Her heart dropped. She truly did not want to go to King Herbert—it was only the principle of the matter. But now it seemed she would have to, due to pride alone. Why must she make such a spectacle of herself?

"You may go," Terrance continued. "However, I will accompany you."

She grinned. She should kick him in the shins, but instead she looked into his shining brown eyes and smiled like a fool. He was so good to her!

"Ahem." Corlan cleared his throat. "Or I could send a trustworthy servant to the battlefront with a letter explaining all and you two could search for Snow instead."

Terrance and Raven looked over at Corlan and laughed.

"He is brilliant," Raven said.

"Thank you. I have my moments." Corlan rose and sighed. "Though I wish I could go after her and see that she is safe. This is killing me, tearing me up inside, knowing she is out there alone and running—running from *me*. I am the monster who plagues her nightmares!"

Oh, dear. Raven stepped forward and hugged him. She could tell her brother was as frazzled as he could be. "Corlan, it is not your fault. No one blames you for this."

"It does not change the fact that it has happened. What if this never goes away? What if one day I *must* kill her? What if I am caught off my guard and follow through with the deed before I can stop myself? Do you know what this does to me, knowing I am the cause of all her sorrows?"

"Shh…" she whispered as she held him tighter. "You need sleep. I do not believe you have had any for quite some time." Her gaze searched Terrance's eyes over her brother's shoulder, asking for help.

"Corlan?" Terrance placed his hand on her brother's shoulder and pulled them apart. "I think it is a good thing that you stay here. I believe you may be the one to solve the riddle of the mirror. The mirror's owners have never been saved before, but that does not mean it is impossible. Mayhap the queen could be brought out of it. Mayhap she could destroy the mirror herself." The two princes stared at one another before Corlan nodded and Terrance continued, "Do not ever give up hope. If you could fight against this spell and save Snow as you did, anything is possible. It is when we give up that things begin to fall around us."

Corlan took a deep breath and clasped Terrance's arm. "You are correct. There is much I can do here as well. And I will not give up on my mother—I can't."

Raven looked at Terrance as the men released each other and he patted Corlan on the back. They all knew it was useless, but how kind of him to see that her brother needed purpose or he would go mad. And this, this impossible feat, was just the thing to keep his mind centered and staying one step ahead the curse.

Prince Terrance was truly a unique man, one who did things to her heart that she never thought possible.

She glanced at her bother and said quite honestly, "Corlan, if anyone has the skill and strategy to defeat this curse, it is you. I believe you will be more successful than any of us can see at this time."

"Thank you. Be safe." He grinned. "And listen to Terrance."

She gasped.

"Yes, I know. You are more than capable of caring for us all, but still, at least *think* of listening to him."

She grinned. "*Perhaps* I will think about it."

Terrance put his arm around her shoulders as he spoke with Corlan. "We will return every couple of days to check in and see that all is well here. I hope to locate Snow quickly and get her to a safe place, a place we will be sure you do not know of until it is time to bring her home." Looking down at Raven, he asked, "Are you ready?" Then his eyes became serious as he said, "You are certain you can handle this?"

If she could not deal with a few nights in the woods, how could she expect her dearest friend to survive? It was ludicrous to remain in this castle another moment when Snow was alone. "Most definitely. Let us begin at once."

CHAPTER NINETEEN

AFTER RAVEN AND TERRANCE left in search of Snow, Corlan sat down in King Herbert's study and wrote out the pressing letter explaining everything that had taken place since the king's departure. He urged his stepfather to think about how best to deal with it all, even explaining his own fears for the king's safety if he returned and his own personal curse to kill Snow. He also let the king know that Prince Terrance and Raven were hoping to find Snow shortly and get her to a place of safety until they heard word from the king on what to do next.

The only part of the tale Corlan did not include was that of Melantha turning into an old woman. He was not certain how to tell the king that his bride was now hideous.

Writing the letter was definitely not a task he would wish upon himself again. It was painful, but it was a relief to see the letter riding off with the stable lad toward the kingdom's borders.

Afterward, he went in search of his mother. When she could not be found in her rooms, he allowed the exhaustion and stress of the past twenty-four hours to descend upon him. Maybe now would be a good time to relax for a bit and catch up on his sleep. He could deal with his mother later.

As he walked up the corridor to his quarters, he could actually feel the fatigue settling upon him like a thick, warm blanket. Every step he took seemed slower and heavier than the last. He must have been much more tired than he imagined. Stumbling into his rooms, he fell upon his bed. Curling up within the blue-and-silver duvet, he snuggled into his pillow and promptly fell asleep.

A few moments later, there was a loud pounding upon his door. "Corlan! Allow me entrance at once!" his mother shrieked on the other side.

He jolted upward, amazed at how dark his room was. How long had he slept? Groggy, his brain could not fathom the time difference. It felt only a few seconds had passed, but it must have been hours.

"Corlan!" she shouted again. "Are you in there? Johnson said you have been in there all night, but if you have not been, I shall hang him as well as everyone else in this house! Now answer me!"

"I am here," he croaked. "I need a minute to sort myself, Mother. You have woken me up."

"It is well I have! I am not pleased at all."

Oh, great heavens. She has found a mirror. He groaned as he rubbed his face and slipped out of bed. What should he do? And then he grinned. It served her right, really. She needed to know how he truly felt about all this.

He straightened his rumpled clothing and opened the door. Melantha's hideous features caused him to jolt a bit in fright. He had forgotten how awful she really looked. "Yes?" he asked.

"Follow me," she commanded and then turned sharply on her heel.

Corlan closed the door and walked the length of the castle following her to her rooms. She flicked at her few balding wisps of hair as if they were indeed thick and flowing as he came to her door. When he entered, he heard the click of the lock and tried unsuccessfully to keep the feeling of fear at bay. What would she do to him now? How many more people would she try to make him kill?

He swallowed and pressed his lips together.

"Come to the mirror, Corlan, dear," she commanded. "I have something I wish to show you."

Bracing himself for the worst, he walked to the mirror and stood beside her.

"Mirror! Show yourself to my son."

Green smoke began to pour out of the frame and then a man's face appeared before them.

"Mirror, mirror on the wall,

Thou claimed I would become fairest of all.

Tell me, my mirror, at this time,

Is the title of 'fairest' truly mine?"

Corlan flinched at the eerie-sounding voice that came from the man. It was a sound he was not familiar with, but it had great distinction in its depths, a commanding yet shivering sort of tone.

"My fair queen, an injustice has been served. You believed your son to be true to your wishes, but I am to tell you that Snow White lives on. She is in a cottage with seven goodly fairies, being pampered and cared for as she has always been. Your son has played a devious trick upon you, for he has given you the heart of a pig to partake of its beauty. You, my fair queen, are fair no longer."

"What? Show me what I look like. Show me now!"

"I can't. I can only reflect how you wish to see yourself and not who you truly are."

She turned to Corlan. "What did you do to me? Can you see my true features?"

He nodded.

"And have you made your mother hideous?"

"You wanted me to kill Snow! You wanted to eat her heart! You wanted her beauty for yourself and I am supposed to allow such a thing? Mother, can you even hear the words coming from your mouth? Can you process what you have truly become? Your actions have only allowed you to show on the outside how repulsive you have become. You can't hide what is inside you any longer."

She lunged forward and grabbed his throat. "You will pay for this!" she hissed. "You shall truly know pain now—pain like you have never known before."

He pushed her away. Her body, though strong, was not as strong as it had been before the transformation. "Torture me however you see fit, but I will not perform your evil deeds for you!"

Melantha ran to the mirror and grasped it in desperation. "Mirror, how can I become handsome again? Tell me!"

"Once Snow White is truly dead and gone, you shall receive the glory that once was yours."

"And if I eat her heart?"

"No!" Corlan moved to pull Melantha away from the mirror, but he was frozen again and he could not hear the words the mirror spoke. They conversed for a while, with each second his own breathing becoming more difficult.

"Is it true?" She suddenly whipped her head toward Corlan. "Are you in love with her? Is this why you have defied your mother, because you are enamored with the woman who is set upon destroying us all?"

When she saw he could not move, she demanded of the mirror, "Allow my son to speak."

Corlan wanted to lie, to protect Snow in any way possible, but the words came unbidden from his lips before he could stop them, as if he were being forced to tell only the truth. "Yes, I am in love with her. I love her more than life itself, more than I love anyone—even you."

"Well, well..." She slowly walked around his stiff form. "We are in a quandary, are we not? I want Snow White dead to remove this curse you have put upon me. You need her alive so you can make your own precious heart happy." She leaned in and whispered in his ear. "Thank you. I now know the perfect pain you shall receive as a reward for your betrayal. You will hunt your beloved. Your skills will grow beyond all you have known and you will find this cottage where she lives."

"No!" he forced out. "I will not."

"And you will lead me directly to her, like a hunting dog leads its master to the sly fox. She is your prey, my son. And when I find her, you will know pain unlike anything you have experienced before because you will know it was you who led me to her, you who helped orchestrate her death. And you will witness her choking on poison and gasping her last breaths. I shall guarantee it!"

"You are mad."

"No, my son, the word you are looking for is 'livid.' I am extremely livid right now. And I will not have my plans thwarted because of disobedience." She walked to the mirror. "Give me all I ask. Make Prince Corlan a skilled hunter. Allow his senses to ripen so that he may find her, and allow nothing to shake this from him until she is dead.

See that he does not betray his mother again!"

Corlan struggled against his frozen limbs, but could not budge as the smoke began to rise up his legs. "You are not my mother! You are nothing like that woman!"

Melantha stepped up to him, her haggard features taking on a look of amusement. "No, I am not. I am a simple old farmer woman, peddling some sweet apples for Snow White to try. Thankfully she will never recognize me as I am and will gobble the poisoned fruit so very easily. And you—she will never recognize you, either." She brought out a folded piece of paper from within her pocket.

Corlan gasped. It was the letter he had written to King Herbert. He would never receive it!

"My disloyal son, you shall come as my dog! It is time you proved your loyalty."

CHAPTER TWENTY

SNOW STRETCHED AND AWOKE her second morning in the pretty cottage. Grinning, she looked over the bright room and sighed. They had adorned the whole place with white, yellow, and pink roses. How she loved roses! Even her coverlet upon the bed was quilted white with embroidered pink and yellow roses all over it. It was simply the most cheerful room she had ever been in. Her gracious hosts had also created charming white furniture. As she slipped off the bed and approached the carved wardrobe, she once again marveled at the pretty frocks awaiting her inside.

This was indeed a magical house. Every time she opened the wardrobe doors, there were more new gowns inside for her to select from. My goodness! It was actually a chore to have to decide which one she would wear, knowing she would never see it again and therefore she must make the right choice.

Snow giggled as she pulled out a frothy yellow summer gown. Its wispy sleeves and skirts did much to make her feel feminine as she tugged it over her head and tied its wide white sash. Dipping back inside, she fetched matching yellow slippers and placed them upon her feet.

Friday Joy would be in any moment to do her hair and she wanted to be already dressed when she came. Joy was the yellow-haired fairy and Snow hoped she approved of the dress this morning. Sitting down at the pretty white carved vanity, Snow smiled at her reflection in the looking glass. In such a happy home as this, she had to believe that everything would turn right. How could it not when such magic existed?

At the knock on her door, she called out, "Come in!"

"Well, good morning," Joy chirped as she came into the room, her arms full of roses. "Look what Hope cut for you today. Our garden has been positively brimming with them since you came."

"Has it?"

Joy set the roses on Snow's dresser, her yellow eyes twinkling in the mirror as she glanced over at Snow. "Did you not know that enchanted cottages are designed to make you feel especially at home? You will always eat your most favorite foods, and your favorite flowers will bloom spontaneously to your moods and wishes." She walked over and picked up a brush from the vanity near Snow's elbow. "And since our garden has been full of sweet roses, Hope decided you must want some with you as well."

Snow closed her eyes as the fairy began to brush her long hair. It was a mass of curling tangles whenever she attempted the thing, but with Joy's touch, her hair seemed to flow into sumptuous long ringlets. "Is that why the room décor is done in my favorite colors?"

"Mhmm… And why the wardrobe will provide you with a never-ending supply of your most favorite gowns, even dresses you would not have ever known were your favorite until you tried them on."

"It does spoil me to have so many choices, especially when they are all equally desirable."

"Well, you are Snow White, my dear." Joy grinned as she placed a pretty white rose into her hair, securing it with pins.

Snow shook her head. *My goodness, this much attention toward one girl can't be fine.* "I am just a girl. Nothing more, nothing less."

Joy met her gaze in the mirror. "Does it bother you to be so pampered?"

Snow dropped her gaze a bit. "It has not been an easy life." Her eyes met the fairy's again. "I do not mean that I am ungrateful for it. I only want to clarify that sometimes I would like to know how it would feel to be judged upon my own merit, the integrity of my heart. To have someone love me because they know me, not because of a silly enchantment clouding their perception."

Joy's hands stilled while placing a pink rose next to the white one. "Oh, I see. I have never thought about it that way before." She quickly tucked a few pins around the bottom petals of the rose. "It must be vexing, certainly, never to know if you are actually loved for who you are."

Snow sighed. "It can be painful, yes." Her heart lurched before she confided quietly, "I can't even trust the instincts of the men who come to pay court to me. I do not want to be caught by a man who does not really know me or see me."

Tucking in a yellow rose to form a pretty trio in Snow's hair, Joy said, "You say you can't trust the instincts of men, but have you considered that perchance you are already smitten by one and so can't be bothered to accept the advances of anyone else?"

"Who?" Snow asked as she felt her face turning red. Did Joy know? She refused even to glance at herself in the mirror. She knew how silly she must look.

"And you *do* blush! That is the most color I have seen upon your white skin since you came here."

Snow smiled.

"There is a prince you speak of often, you know." Joy brushed one last ringlet into place and leaned down to hug Snow from behind. "Mayhap he is the one who has already captured your heart."

Biting her lip, Snow met the fairy's eyes in the mirror. "You know, I believe you may be correct."

Joy pushed away from the vanity, laughing a tinkling laugh. "Oh, we fairies are always correct, dear. You pretty human girls can be read quite as easily as any book. Now, look at that glorious hair!"

"Thank you," Snow said as she stood and examined herself. "You do wonders."

"I am only making sure you feel like a princess while you are here, Your Highness."

"Joy?" Turning around, Snow stepped up to her. "Do you think if I asked agreeably, you and your sisters would consider removing this spell from me?" She clasped her hands. "I want to know what it is actually like to live within the world."

Joy looked at her closely and then nodded. "We will discuss the possibility," she promised. "Though, I should warn you. I am not certain they will agree. Your safety is the most important thing to me and my sisters."

"But you will ask them?"

"Yes."

Snow smiled and threw her arms around the beautiful woman. "Thank you! That would make me the happiest.""

"Are you certain? Joy teased. "Not even if perhaps a certain prince were to lose his curse and come waltzing up to our cottage—even that would not make you happier?"

Snow blushed again.

"I thought so!" Joy walked to the door and opened it. "Now I feel like some breakfast."

The smell of delicious buttered honey buns wafted its way down the hallway and into Snow's room. "Oh, I do not think I will ever want to leave this cottage."

"And you did not wish to be spoiled. Ha!" Joy said as she walked out of the room.

"Oh, you mistake me completely. I have no problem being pampered with my choice of delights. Nay, I only wish to come by it all honestly."

"Well, you are honestly loved here, so for now, do not worry about anything else. And enjoy. We guarantee we will keep you safe until your father returns."

CHAPTER TWENTY-ONE

TERRANCE HALTED IN CLEANING up the breakfast things at their campsite in the forest when he heard the sound of a voice coming their way. He quickly threw an arm out to let Raven know there was trouble heading straight for them.

Her eyes flew to his and then she nodded, silently scrambling to put the things into her pack and duck out of sight into a bush.

He quickly tamped down the fire, though there was nothing they could do about the smell. Whoever was coming would know they had been there. He gathered his blankets and pack in a pile and headed through the shrubbery to crouch behind the bush next to Raven.

As the voice drew closer, it sounded like an old woman.

"Stop, you fool dog! Come back here! You have to wait for me."

They heard a whack and then Raven jumped as a dog yelped in response. Terrance placed his arm around her and drew her back a bit farther into the shrubs.

"What do we have here?" the old woman asked as she stepped into their line of view. She carried a covered basket and a little bag.

They remained as silent as possible as she searched around their small campsite.

"Dog, come here. Tell me if you smell Snow White."

Raven covered her gasp with her hand.

"Shh…" Terrance reminded in her ear. Who was this woman? How did she know Snow?

A large brown dog bounded into the area and began sniffing around. It halted on its back legs and then tilted its head before moving and sniffing some more. He came up to their bush, but then after sniffing a few moments, continued on.

"Well? Who has been here?" the woman asked as she prodded the ashes with her cane. "Do you see that smoke? This fire is still hot." She stood straighter and scanned the area, her gaze settling upon the bush where they hid.

Terrance had never seen a more hideous woman in all his life. His arm tightened protectively around Raven. When the old woman began to walk toward them, they stiffened.

"In fact, I do believe they have not gone very far at all," the old woman said, walking ever closer.

Just then the dog barked.

"What is it?" She turned her head. "Have you found Snow White?"

The dog barked again and began to run away from their camp. The old woman was quick to follow. "Corlan!" she shouted. "Get back here. I told you to wait for me!" The dog returned only to receive another whack with the cane. "Now stay with me. And do not proceed faster than I can walk or you will be killed as well. Take me to her. It is time we end this."

Terrance's heart pounded and he could feel Raven's quivering form beneath his arm. In the tight space, they looked at each other. "Melantha and Corlan," he whispered so silently, it was as if he mouthed it.

Her brow furrowed as she pressed her lips together. He could see her eyes shimmering with unshed tears. They could still hear the queen shouting her commands.

He pulled her toward him and allowed Raven to release her emotions into his chest. After her mother's voice grew more distant, he spoke. "Raven, I know how terrifying this must be for you. I am sorry."

"Oh, Corlan and Mother!" She pulled back and sniffed as she wiped her eyes. "What has become of them? I abhor that cursed mirror! I despise it!"

"I know."

"Why, oh why must it be a part of us? Why must it destroy everything I love?"

How he wished he could take this from her. "I know."

"And now they are after Snow!" She put her hand over his mouth. "And if you say 'I know' one more time, I will throttle you."

He grinned beneath her hand. "I know."

Raven rolled her eyes and pushed his shoulder. "You are so aggravating." She sighed. "Now what do we do?"

He brushed off her harsh words and answered, "Well, I say we stay out of sight and track them, letting them lead us to Snow."

"Is there a way out of this mess?"

He placed his hand on her shoulder. "Yes. I promise there is."

She shook her head, a flash of irritation going across her features. "Terrance, do not humor me. I am not in the mood to be humored."

"I am *not* humoring you!" He stood up, his own flare of anger at her easy dismissal coursing through him. As quickly as possible, he folded the rest of their blankets and shoved them in his pack. Picking up her pack as well, he said, "Let us go." Then he stepped from behind the bush, ready to put some distance between them.

"Wait, Terrance!"

He turned. She looked so lost and confused and agitated.

"Forgive me," she said.

He could tell she was pulled as tight as she could get, her fragile hold stretched to the limit. "Come." He held his arm out, not able to bear seeing her this way. "There is nothing to forgive."

"No." She did not budge. "I have been discourteous to you over and over again, and I need to stop. I *will* stop. This is not your affair, this is not your fault—none of it is! And yet, you remain to help me through it, although I continuously barb and wound you. I am truly sorry. Please forgive me?"

Did he hear her properly? Was his Raven admitting fault and accepting that her actions were harmful?

"I am truly sorry," she said again.

My great heavens! Terrance knew then that he loved her, that he would always love her. He retraced his steps and wrapping her up in his arms, he kissed her like he had never kissed her before. When he pulled back slightly, he said, "My dear, thank you."

Her mouth was such a sweet O of surprise that he had to kiss it again. When he pulled back a second time she grinned, her eyes sparkling. She clearly forgot all their troubles for a moment. "If that is what you do when a girl apologizes to you, how much fun it will be to beg your forgiveness continuously."

A chuckle escaped from him. "Are you saying you mean to plague me forever just so we can make up afterward?"

She stepped back and raised an eyebrow, giving him an arch look. "Precisely."

CHAPTER TWENTY-TWO

SNOW LAUGHED AS SHE kissed the cheeks of Monday Truth and Wednesday Love. All the fairies were on their way to prepare the area for the coming autumn. —Changing leaves, adding the sparkling frost, encouraging the fall flowers to bloom. They were supposed to have left a quarter of an hour ago, but they'd hemmed and hawed within the doorway instead. They were such mother hens.

"Now remember to stay inside the cottage while we are away," Love said as she tucked her long red hair behind her ears.

Truth's enchanting silver eyes captured hers. "You are welcome to cook anything you wish or do any sort of activity, like paint, or read, or whatever, as long as it is done in the home."

"Yes, I promise, I will not leave the house!" Snow said for the hundredth time. "All shall be well. You will see."

Grace frowned slightly. "I do not know. For some reason I do not feel at ease leaving you here alone. And yet, we can't do what we must if we bring you."

"Do you really not feel this is wise?" asked Peace, her blue eyes concerned.

Taking a deep breath, Grace answered, "I do not know. No. Yes. Mayhap I am just too overprotective of her."

Peace wrapped an arm around Snow. "If she locks the door and does not go out, no one can come in, either."

"Aye!" Truth said. "It is correct. With the magic over the cottage, no one can come into this home unless one of us lets them in. You know this. We all know this."

Joy frowned. "I feel uneasy as well. Grace is not the only one."

Snow smiled. "Whatever you decide is fine. But I vow not to allow anything harmful to come in here."

Brave sighed. "We have already lost three days' worth of autumn preparedness. If we do not hurry, the farmers may not have the harvests they planned this year."

"What if just one of us stays behind?" Love asked. "Could we make up the work for them together?"

"I could stay home," Hope said. "My chore is the fastest in the fall, as it is just allowing the green to leave. I am not attempting to make things grow."

"Very well." Grace nodded. "Tuesday Hope shall stay here and watch over Snow."

The fairies smiled and Joy took a deep breath. "I feel better already," she said. "And now do you see why we can't release the spell just yet?"

Snow shook her head. "Is this where I tell you I'm just fine and will be perfectly fine on my own?

The fairies groaned.

"Though I'm very happy to have the company of Hope with me."

Grace tittered. "We promise as soon as you're safe, we'll remove it. Does that help?"

"So, after the Lythereon mirror is destroyed?"

"Possibly." Joy shrugged.

"Tis the best we can do." Brave patted her arm.

"Go, shoo!" Snow giggled as she opened the door and began to gently push them out. "I shall be safe. Hope and I will get into lots of mischief and maybe have a surprise for you when you get back."

The women transformed into tiny fairies the second they stepped outside. Taking on their naturally small forms and spreading their gossamer wings, they hovered and waited.

Grace was the last to leave. "Lock this door," she said to Hope and then, turning to Snow, said, "We love you so much. Be ever vigilant."

Snow kissed her cheek. "I will. Thank you. Thank you for everything."

With that, Grace stepped outside and twinkled into a stunning fairy again. "We will be home soon," she called as they flew off.

"So what would you like to do for their surprise?" Hope asked as she locked the door behind them.

"Do you really have paints?" Snow asked. She would love to create something for the empty wall in the parlor.

"Certainly. I will get them." Hope grinned. "And afterward we can make some apple pie for supper. I know you have been asking, and today is the perfect day to show you how they are made."

"Today is wonderful!" Snow could not believe she was as happy as she was. Quite truthfully, she was positive she did not deserve such goodness in her life. If only she could share it with Corlan and the others.

The women toiled away for a few hours with the paints. Snow created a stunning vase of roses on a stretched piece of canvas and Hope repainted an old wooden box, creating a pretty woodland scene upon it.

As they were finishing up, there was a knock upon the door.

Hope glanced over and her eyebrows rose. "Who could that be?"

Snow's stomach dropped. "Perhaps we should pretend we are not here."

"You are very wise." Hope snapped her fingers, and instantly the table cleared. Brushes and paints were tucked back into the closet and their projects were drying on the kitchen counter. "We will go to the back parlor," she said.

"Hello?" called an old woman with a kindly voice. "Hello? Is anyone there?"

Hope froze as a shadow fell across the kitchen. The woman was staring at them from the open window at the side of the house.

"Oh!" said the old woman. "There you are! May I come in and rest my weary feet? I have been traveling for miles when I happened upon this cottage. Thank goodness you are here. I am simply exhausted."

Snow looked at Hope. How could they resist?

The fairy took a deep breath and unlocked the door. "Come in," she said. "Come rest yourself at our table. Oh! And you have a dog with you."

"Yes. Do you mind overly much if he comes in? He is extremely obedient."

"I, uh…" Hope glanced at Snow, who shrugged. "I supposed it will be fine."

The old woman hobbled into the house. Spying a chair in the kitchen, she promptly sat down upon it. Snow watched as her large dog hesitated before coming into the home. He stepped over the threshold and then hunched down near the door, his eyes staring intently at Snow.

"My! You are a pretty little thing," the woman exclaimed as if she had just noticed Snow.

"Thank you."

"My dear," Hope said, "Could you please fetch our guest some water and perhaps a few scones?"

"Oh, that would be lovely." The woman smiled, revealing blackened teeth.

Snow quickly did as she was asked and set the food upon the table.

"Come here." The woman beckoned to her.

All at once the dog growled from the doorway.

"On second thought, perhaps it is best if my dog stays outside," the woman said.

Hope opened the door again, but the dog would not move.

"Go!" commanded the woman a little too fiercely.

Jumping to his feet, the dog barked wildly, staring right at Snow. Strangely, she was not afraid of him. It was not as if he was attempting to scare her. It was more of an insistent bark of some kind.

"You will obey me!" the woman shouted, her shrill voice ringing through the cottage.

The dog whimpered, his eyes looking as though he were pleading with Snow. Was he trying to say something to her?

"He is fine, I am sure," Snow said. "Are you hungry, boy? Is that what you wish to say?" She quickly went into the kitchen and collected a couple of scones for him and a bowl of water before the old woman could object. Walking over, she placed both in front of him, but he did not look down. Instead, he kept his gaze directly upon her. "What? What are you attempting to convey to me?"

He whimpered and nudged her hand.

"Yes?" she asked as she turned it over for him to sniff.

He began to lick it.

"Enough!" shouted the woman. "Get out of this house now!"

The dog gave one bark at Snow and then ran out the open door.

Concerned for him, Snow collected the water and scones and followed him outside. "Here you go. Now you can have something too."

She set the bowl on the ground and then gasped when she saw his paw drawing a design on the ground. It almost looked like a letter. She turned to the side. It *was* a letter! An R. Glancing at him, she noticed he was already writing something else—U. And then another—N. RUN.

She met his gaze then. What was he trying to say? "Run? I should run?"

The dog barked.

Snow's heart began to pound. "Are you under a spell?"

The dog barked again and looked at the letters upon the ground.

"You want me to run? Why? What is it?"

"Oh, dear!" the old woman called from the door. "Is he playing his RUN game with you? He just loves that game

213

so much! He must really like you to include you in it." She wagged a finger at the dog. "No, no, sir! She does not have time to play your games with you. And you are in trouble for barking anyhow." Then her voice changed significantly. In a haunting chant she said, "You will obey me and never bark again!" She pointed her finger at him until he cowed and whimpered. When he was lying upon the ground with his head between his paws as if he were frozen, the old woman smiled and then beckoned to Snow. "Now come here, dearie. I have a gift for you." Her voice was sweet as she held out a shiny red apple. "I have already given one to your charming friend. Now this one is for you."

Almost in a trance, Snow felt her feet move toward the old woman. The apple did look so good. All at once, she was very hungry and felt as if nothing but that apple could satisfy her. She extended her hand as she approached and felt the weight of the fruit fall into her palm. Before she was fully aware of what was happening, she brought her hand up and bit into the delicious apple and felt its sweet juice running down her chin.

CHAPTER TWENTY-THREE

NO! CORLAN WHIMPERED AS he watched Snow drop the apple.

She turned and clutched at her chest. The pretty yellow gown twisted in her hands as she gasped for air.

How he wished he could move! How he wished he could run to her side. Melantha had frozen him as he watched on in horror. She was right. He had never known pain such as this.

Never.

Snow collapsed. Her shoulders and head pounded into the dirt and the ground crushed the roses in her hair. Still attempting to breathe, her eyes met his as she choked and lunged for air.

No! No!

I am so sorry, Snow! I am so sorry!

Melantha laughed as Snow took her final wheeze before her eyes closed and she became still. Instantly his mother transformed into the red-haired beauty she had been before.

"She is gone! Snow White is forever gone!" She snickered with glee and then grinned as she walked over to the stiff Corlan. "Well, my boy. Do you feel the pain now? Do you?" She kicked him in the ribs and he yelped. "I hope you learned your lesson!" she hissed. "I will leave you here with your dead princess to remember always."

She snapped her fingers and he felt the transformation commence, bringing him back to his true form. The night before, she had insisted the mirror give her power to do this. Now she had become as powerful as a witch.

"Good-bye, son."

Lying on the ground, he waited until she had left and then crawled over to Snow and gently picked her up. He placed her head within his lap. "Snow," he whispered to her as he brushed aside the dirty hair from her face. She was so beautiful. It was not fair! How could he have lost her?

Pulling her in closer, he brought her head to his chest and rocked.

No. No. No.

This was not fair.

How could he have brought his mother here? Why did he not try harder to withstand the curse? His shoulders shook as his lips brushed her forehead. *I am sorry, Snow. I am so, so sorry.*

"I needed you," he whispered into her brow. "I needed you. Your laughter, your sweetness, your smile. I have never known a girl as kind as you. I know you felt it was all an enchantment, but I promise you my dear, I loved you before anyone saw you. I loved you all those years ago when we played together and laughed together. I knew then my heart would never be the same." He cried. "Forgive me for never telling you, for pretending you did not matter as much as you did. You should have heard my admiration. You should have known it. I was a fool to believe you had heard it too much from the other men."

So busy was he in proclaiming the words Snow never got to hear, he did not realize the fairy was upon him until he felt her hand touch his shoulder.

Startled, he looked up to see the woman with bright turquoise hair and eyes. "You did not eat the apple?" he asked, positive Melantha had told Snow she had given her one.

"Yes, I did." She smiled sadly, her eyes scanning Snow's lifeless form in his arms. "But I am a fairy—we are exempt from dark magic. It can wound us for a time, but we can't be defeated. I have called the others, and they should be here shortly. We will see what they can do."

Could it be true? Dare he allow his heart to hope there was a cure for this? What if it did not work? "Can you help her, then? Can you bring her back?"

"I do not know. None of us have ever faced anything so dire as a Lythereon Mirror curse."

She knelt down and ran a hand over Snow's face. "She is remarkably stunning, even in death," she whispered.

Corlan nodded and blinked back a few tears. "I can't bear the thought of her being gone. Please, if you know of anything that may work—any legend, anything—I will attempt it. Even giving up my own soul so that she might be free." He brightened. "Is it possible? Could you trade my life for hers?"

"No." She shook her head. "The mirror has already exchanged her life for your mother's beauty. The Lythereon Mirror is powerful, but cunning as well. It will never allow its masters to receive *everything* they desire, or they would become more powerful than it."

Just then several bright lights appeared and transformed themselves into enchanting human-sized women.

"Snow is gone!" the lavender-haired one exclaimed. "No! I felt something dreadful would happen, but not this! Look, sisters, her light has left. She is deceased."

The women murmured.

"Who are you?" demanded the green-haired one, her face taking on a look of anger as she noticed Corlan. "Did you kill her?"

"No. I am Prince Corlan. Who are you?"

"Saturday Brave." And then she gasped. "Why, it is you! You are the prince cursed by the mirror."

"Yes."

The yellow fairy suddenly smiled. "You are the one she spoke of so fondly."

"She spoke of me?" he asked. Why were they all smiling?

The turquoise fairy reached over and grasped his hand. "My dear, did I overhear correctly? Are you in love with our Snow?"

She looked so eager and joyful. They all did. "Yes, of course I am. Why? Am I missing something?"

The red woman laughed and clapped her hands. "I am Wednesday Love," she said. "And we are so excited because it means I can possibly bring her back!"

"What?" His heart began to pound. "What do you mean?"

"We believe Snow is in love with you as well," said the silver fairy. "I am Monday Truth, and I would bargain wings on the truth that she is in love with you."

"Me?" Warmth fissured through his frame. "Are you certain? She never claimed to have loved anyone."

"No," said the turquoise woman, "but we have hope."

He looked down at Snow, his eyes caressing her features. "What should I do? What do you need from me?"

Love knelt beside him and ran a hand from Snow's hair to her toes as the other women leaned around them in a circle to watch. Corlan glanced up at Love as she spoke.

"Hold her right wrist with your right hand. Just like so," she said as she clasped Snow's left wrist. "Now hold my other hand."

"Very well."

She muttered a few words and he felt an energy surge through his arms and chest, going round and round, circling through all three of them. Once he felt the energy pulse begin to quicken, she said, "Now kiss her! For only true love can break darkness such as this."

He leaned down, his eyes going to her soft red lips. Did she truly love him? Could it be possible? Would this really work? He felt the pulse quicken even more as the power of Love coursed through him and he lowered his mouth to hers.

CHAPTER TWENTY-FOUR

A BRIGHT LIGHT EXPLODED and Corlan's lips molded more firmly to Snow's. As the light dissipated, his lips released their hold and he pulled back.

"Please work," he whispered. "Please come back to me."

Just then her chest rocked forward and she gasped.

"It worked!" he exclaimed as he watched her eyes flutter open and her breathing become normal.

She blinked and then slowly grinned. "Hello."

"Well, hello yourself," he said.

"You are here."

"You are back."

Snow tugged free of his and Love's hands to reach up and place her arms around Corlan's shoulders. "Did you just kiss me awake, like in the fairy stories?"

"Aye, I did." He chuckled. "When you are with fairies and they tell you to do something, you'd better do it."

Snow looked around the group above them before looking back at him. "I feel different now. Is something different? Has the enchantment I've been under been lifted?"

Brave gasped. "Of course, it was broken the second Melantha came to harm you."

Corlan looked at them funny. "It can't be broken. I still feel the pull for her."

Love gave a rueful grin. "That's because you are her true love."

"I did wake you, didn't I?" Corlan's gaze traveled over her face.

"Precisely." Truth grinned.

Snow smiled and then asked, "How long have I been asleep?"

He shook his head. "It was worse than that. You were not asleep. Melantha poisoned you."

"The apple?"

"Yes."

Her lively eyes sparkled at him. "But you are not cursed anymore? You are not trying to kill me?"

How grateful it was to see her and feel her again. "No." He blinked as he realized this was true. "I have been released!"

"As have I. So what are you waiting for?" she whispered, her eyes searching his.

"What do you mean?"

"Well, are you not going to kiss me again? Now that we are both back to normal?"

"Minx." He laughed. "You would not mind? Are you sure it is me you are in love with and not all those other handsome men?"

She rolled her eyes and tugged him toward her.

"Wait." He placed a hand over her mouth and glanced up at the delighted women. "Do you mind giving us a just a bit of privacy?"

They playfully groaned and snickered amongst themselves before turning around and walking away. Even Love stood up. "We will be in the cottage, where Hope will fill us in on all that happened here. You two enjoy yourselves."

"Thank you!" Corlan said.

She winked in reply and then went in the home with the others.

"Now, where were we?" he asked.

"You were about to kiss me senseless."

Corlan's eyebrows rose. "I was? Are you sure?"

Snow giggled. "Yes. Perfectly sure."

And so, he did just that, kissing her like he had imagined doing for ages now. They would more than likely still be kissing today, so enjoyable they found it, if they were not interrupted by Raven and Terrance bursting out from the rose garden.

"Snow!" Raven called. "Snow, where are you?"

Corlan heard Terrance answer, "There she is. See? In Corlan's arms."

"You are not a dog!" Raven ran up to him.

"I think we have been found." Corlan grinned down at Snow.

She good-humoredly sighed. "Yes. It would seem that way."

He quickly kissed her one more time before helping the beautiful girl to her feet. He brushed at a few stray pieces of debris from her hair as Raven chattered.

"I am so happy to see you both here and alive! We thought for sure when we lost sight of my mother that you would both be dead."

"I was, apparently," Snow said. "Corlan brought me back, though."

"Thankfully Melantha removed the curse or no one would have known it was me."

"Where is she now?" Terrance asked.

Corlan shook his head. "After she poisoned Snow and transformed back into her former self, she left. I do not know if she walked or simply disappeared and went back to the castle. I was too worried about Snow to care where my mother had gone."

"Have you heard from King Herbert?" Terrance asked.

"No. The letter I wrote never made it to him—she took it. Hence the reason she transformed me into a dog—to make me prove my loyalty to her."

"I need to find a horse and get to him immediately. Someone needs to let him know what is happening," Terrance said.

Snow spoke up. "I believe they are discussing the matter in full detail at the moment. The fairies who have been watching over me are not a group to be messed with. I think they expect to battle the mirror."

"Wait. Fairies?" Raven asked. "You have been living here, in this gorgeous cottage, with fairies?"

Snow nodded. "Oh, goodness, I have so much to show you! Let us go inside and see what their plan of attack may be. You will be amazed at how magical they are."

"Do you believe we could get Mother back?" Raven asked as they began to walk toward the house.

Corlan nudged Terrance before he began following them inside. "I have begun to see what you mean."

"What?" Terrance asked.

"About women." He waggled his eyebrows and glanced at Snow as she walked into the cottage on Raven's arm, her long black ringlets tempting him with every bounce. "I am quite smitten."

"And would you do anything for her?"

"Anything."

Terrance grinned and nodded as he began to follow them. "Aye. It is always about the women."

"Yes, it is," Corlan said as they stepped into the cottage. "And thank goodness, or life would be excessively boring."

CHAPTER TWENTY-FIVE

THE FAIRIES WELCOMED SNOW and the rest in with bounteous food and laughter around the enlarged table. The group introduced themselves properly and they discussed at length what would be the best plan of attack against Melantha and her powerful mirror. Everyone was unanimous in agreeing that she must be stopped at all costs. Too many lives were at stake, and already she had complete control over King Herbert's castle. Soon, she would control all of Olivian.

"I think it is wise for Terrance to head to King Herbert as soon as possible," Grace said. "Let the king know the threat that is within his home."

Brave and Peace both agreed.

"I will guarantee you arrive quickly and safely," Peace said.

Brave added, "And you will be protected. I see him fighting a great battle at the moment, though I believe it has been brought on by the mirror. If we can destroy that mirror, I feel the threat of war will cease."

"So do I," Peace said. "It is why we need you to get to Herbert and let him know all."

Terrance nodded. "I will leave at once."

"Truth will create a swift horse for you. One that will get you there extremely fast so you will be able to meet us at the castle by nightfall," Grace said.

"So it is to be tonight?" asked Snow. Already the butterflies in her stomach were beating wildly, but she found herself more eager to face the queen than to hide. It was time she did her part to save Olivian from their new queen.

"Yes." Corlan folded his arms. "The quicker my mother is stopped, the fewer people will be harmed. It must be tonight."

"We will travel by fairyflight." Grace looked at Terrance. "As soon as Herbert is on his way, we will arrange it so we arrive just a bit before him to create the surprise needed to catch Melantha off guard."

"Would it be easier if I traveled with the prince and then sounded the horn when we were about a quarter of an hour away?" Brave asked.

"Perfect!" Joy exclaimed.

"Yes, go," Grace said. "It will ensure that nothing goes wrong."

Terrance and Brave stood from the table and waited for Truth to come around from the other end. The prince leaned down and left a quick, surprising kiss on Raven's lips. "Be safe," he said to her.

"Me? But you are the one going to the battlefront."

"Yes, you. Be safe." He grinned. "I want to taste those lips again when I return tonight."

"Ha! We will see if you deserve another kiss."

"If you did not grin I would believe your protests, but since I can tell you are as eager as I am, I guarantee you will get your wish."

Raven flushed and the group laughed as he walked outside with the fairies.

"What will you need me to do?" Snow asked, eager to help in any way she could.

Grace turned to Corlan. "What do you feel would be best for her?"

Corlan glanced over Snow and then said, "My mother thinks Snow is dead. We can use that to our advantage. What can you fairies do to help us stop Melantha? Right now, the magic of the mirror halts me, completely freezes my limbs so I must do what it requires of me. I am overpowered. Is there a way to somehow trap her before she can overpower us?"

"Yes!" Peace exclaimed. "There is. If we are all together, we should be able to trap her in her own magic, which would mean locking her within the mirror. But all of us must be together to do so."

"How does it work?" Snow asked.

Grace spoke up. "When we were created, we were intended to be a force—an opposition against evil. And therefore, each of our gifts, our names, are interlinked. You can't oppose evil without our characteristics. Once you have all seven within you, all seven days of the week, you can withstand anything the opposition throws your way.

"Each of our days are significant as well, but I will not go into all of that. Suffice it to say, with the Grace of the Almighty, the Truth you can withstand all, the Hope life will get better, Love over everything, Peace which dwells within, Joy at life and all her ups and downs, and Bravery—the ability to face it all without fear. Once you have us all together, there is nothing the opponent can do to you. It is simply trapped. But if you allow one of these gifts to fade, you welcome the enemy in."

"Just think," Joy said. "Think of what she is saying. What if you did not have Truth or Hope, but you had the others? You could not fully trap your enemy. You must have Joy and Peace as well. You must have it all. And once you have mastered that, you can defeat anything."

"It would seem the mirror is based on the opposite qualities," Corlan said. "It is all about greed, envy, strife, murder, fear, lies …"

"Yes, and now do you see why it was imperative that we watched over Snow like we did?"

"I am so very grateful you promised my mother you would," she said. "Who knew how much I would actually need you now?"

Hope smiled. "Life has an interesting way of coming full circle.

Indeed, you never know who will turn out to be the exact person you need in your life. When you first meet them, you can't imagine what role they may end up playing. It is something I find quite fascinating."

Corlan stood up and began to pace within the parlor.

Snow could tell he would not rest until the full strategy had worked itself out within his mind. She listened to the fairies' chatter for a few minutes before walking over to him. "What are you thinking?" she asked.

He stopped and glanced her way. "I was just pondering everything, wondering if perhaps this might actually work. Remember, I have read the accounts of what the mirror has done in the other kingdoms. We must at least try to withstand it."

"None of the other kingdoms had fairies," she said.

"I know. It is what gives me hope." He grinned over in Hope's direction.

Snow searched his features until he looked at her again. Then she caught his gaze and held it. "Do you believe Melantha can come back to us?" she whispered.

Corlan closed his eyes briefly. "I hope so, though I do wonder how we will ever be able to forgive her."

She looked at him for a while and could not say a word. Even her forgiving heart would take a long time to trust and forgive after this.

"Come you two," Grace called. "Let us sort through the rest of our plans. No matter what happens tonight, whether we are able to save Melantha or not, our true focus is to bring peace back to Olivian and remove the curse from the castle."

They planned for several hours, all of them together. The fairies made sure everyone was comfortable and well fed, but the plan was all anyone could speak of. And then just around seven o'clock, Love announced to the group, "I hear the horn. It is time!"

Quickly, Raven, Corlan, and Snow huddled together while four fairies stood around them, tugging upon their clothes.

Snow looked up at Corlan, her hands clenched his. Her slight fear must have shown on her face because he kissed her brow and whispered, "It will be fine. I will not allow her to harm you."

"Now!" Grace commanded. "It is time."

And they were gone.

CHAPTER TWENTY-SIX

THE GROUP ARRIVED JUST outside the castle. As they had planned earlier, Corlan walked in alone first while the others waited for King Herbert and Brave to appear. He made his way directly to his mother's rooms. If all went as intended, they might manage to trap her within the mirror. What happened after that was still uncertain, but at least a massive battle would not be needed, thanks to the help of the fairies. It was crucial that the fewest people possible be harmed in this confrontation.

He knocked upon her door. "Mother, I have come home."

The door opened on its own and he found her seated in front of her mirror, her back to him, her red hair as full and pretty as before.

"I know," she stated simply. "I know everything."

He walked closer to her as she flicked her wrist and the door slammed shut. "Are you sure you know everything?"

"Yes!" she hissed and turned toward him. She was even more hideous than before.

He flinched. Her face had a green-grayish tint to it with deep lines and a long, crooked nose. "Mother?"

"Yes, Corlan, it is I, your mother." She stood from her chair and took a few steps toward him, her back greatly bowed. "This is what you made me! This is the monster I have become now!" Her eyes took on a reddish hue. "Do you see me?"

"How did *I* do this?" he asked.

She shrieked and lunged for him, her nails like pointed claws. But he easily sidestepped her. When she fell to the ground, he did not offer to help her up. "Do you see this? Do you see me?" she wailed. "I found the mirrors you hid away. I have seen myself, and it is your fault! You and your precious Snow White!"

She let out a wild roar at Snow's name, her face contorting as she howled at the ceiling. "I want her *dead!*" she screamed. *"Dead!"* Her breathing became harsh afterward and she had to speak softer. "Why did you bring her back to life? Why did you work with those dim-witted fairies? You had to fall under Snow's spell, just like everyone else." She reached for a stool near his feet and threw it upward at him.

He dodged just as it whizzed past his head.

"Why were you so stupid? Did you not know what she was doing to you? You do not love her! You would never love her on your own. She has forced it out of you!" Melantha lay down and curled into a ball as she began to sob. "Look what it has done to me. Your own mother."

"No," he said quietly. "It was not Snow's curse that has ruined everything." He hunched down to be closer to her. "It is your greed and your mirror that have destroyed you. You chose this life. You chose this *face*. I have no sympathy for anyone who cares so little about the people they rule over that they would follow the promptings of an evil mirror."

"Take it back, Corlan," she said, her voice taking on an eerie quality.

"Never." He stood up. "I will never, for it is the truth! Your greed has given you this appearance. I am only attempting to save this kingdom from you before it is too late!"

"Take it back, Corlan." Her shoulders began to shake.

He stepped further away. "No. You need to hear the truth before all is lost. We can save you. We have come to save you, Mother. If you destroy the mirror, everything will go back to the way it was. Everything. But *you* must do it! You must!"

"I will never destroy that mirror!" she screeched. In a great flurry of motion, she stood up and began to grow before him, rising higher and higher.

"You must!" he shouted at her.

"The mirror is me!" Her features blurred briefly and on her shoulders he saw the mirror's face—a man peering down at him. "We are one!" she bellowed, her voice echoing wildly.

Just then the fairies broke through the door.

"No, you demon!" Corlan ran toward her. "Get out of her! You do not own Melantha!"

"Corlan! Halt!" Terrance shouted as he rushed into the room. "Do not attack the mirror or it will absorb you too!"

Melantha grew even taller. Her red wig slipped off, showing scales down her neck.

Corlan stepped back, coming flush up to Raven and Snow. "Get out of this room!" he fiercely whispered.

"No. I came to face this with you," Snow said.

Terrance pushed Raven behind him and moved her toward the door as the small fairies went forward.

"I know all!" the queen said. "I know why you are here! You wish to kill me! You want to demolish my mirror. I will not let you! You will all die first!" Green smoke began to pour into the room—from her mouth this time.

"Now!" shouted Corlan to the fairies. "Do it now!"

The fairies formed a circle in the air as the green smoke lapped up Corlan's legs, freezing him to the spot just as King Herbert ran into the rooms and became frozen as well.

The fairies chanted something and the whole chamber glowed in a mystical white light before it flashed—the brightness exceeding anything Corlan had ever experienced before.

All at once, he could hear the sound of Melantha shrieking, and he noticed he could move his arms. "It worked! The power is receding!" Twisting around, he saw the others moving their arms too. The fairies were now above Melantha, and she had shrunk back to her normal size. The green smoke seemed to be pulling her into the mirror with it.

The queen's frantic shrieks pinged in his ears. As the smoke slid down his legs, he could feel his knees and then feet give way. Finally he was free! He spun around and captured Snow quickly up to his heart. "Do not leave my side," he whispered in her ear, grateful she was still in one piece.

"Melantha, enough!" shouted King Herbert as she slipped into the mirror. He ran up to the looking glass.

Her hideous face peered at him in shock. "Herbert?"

"I am here!" His eyes traced her features anxiously. "What have you done, my dear? What have you done?"

"Do not look at me!" She hid behind her hands in the looking glass. "Go away! Leave me now!"

Corlan stepped forward. This was the mother he remembered. Could the curse be slipping?

The king grasped the mirror. "What have you done to yourself?"

She peeked at him through her green fingers. "You came back."

"Of course I did! I would always come back for you!"

"The mirror said you would not. He said you would never come back to me, that you hated me." She began to sob, her face still covered.

"Fairies, please release a portion of her, if you can," Herbert said. "Please. Just her head. I wish to speak to her, to touch her."

"No!" Melantha tried to pull away, but the bright light of the fairies' magic forced her head and neck out of the mirror, removing her hands to show them all how truly revolting she had become. The queen turned her head away.

"Herbert, leave me. Do not see me this way, I beg of you." Her sobs grew even more.

"Shh…" The king stepped forward and brushed a tear from her green, lined cheek. "I did not fall in love with your beauty, my dear. I fell in love with your heart, your desire to change the world for good." He held her face and peered into her eyes. "Where is my bride? Where is her heart? I know she is in there. Come back to me."

"Herbert, you fool!" she shouted at him. "I killed your daughter! You do not want me. I will only continue to hunt you all. I am not who I once was!"

"Mirror!" Herbert commanded, "I am speaking to my bride. I want no more of your conversation here. Leave us!" Still holding her face, he said, "Melantha, tell him to leave!"

She shook her head slightly as more tears came. "I can't."

"Yes, you can. It is that easy. He must listen to you. You own him. He does not own you—not yet. Do not let him take you from me. Melantha, I know you are there."

"Why do you care? I am a monster now. You do not love me. You *should not* love me!"

"You are wrong. You are so very wrong. Do not leave me, my dear. Do not allow the mirror to take you too." A tear made its way down the king's face. "Come back. I love you!"

"Herbert?" she cried. "How could you still love me after all this?"

He leaned forward and kissed her green lips as if she really was the dearest woman on earth. "Because I am yours. I have always been yours. And I will not give up on you just because you have given up on yourself. I love you, Melantha. Tell the mirror to leave so I can have you again. I need you, my dear. I need you."

CHAPTER TWENTY-SEVEN

RAVEN WATCHED WITH TEARS rolling down her cheeks as Melantha closed her eyes. She had never truly understood the goodness of her stepfather's heart until that moment. If every woman had the love of a man as great as King Herbert, no woman would ever fail.

She brushed at her tears as Terrance's arm wrapped around her waist and brought her in closer. "Are you well?" he asked.

Sniffling, she nodded. "Yes."

Her mother's face twisted and strained, its ugly features distorting even more. The image of the mirror formed upon her features before flickering away again. "Release me!" she shouted as she pushed against the force of the curse surrounding her. "Release me now!"

All at once, the mirror's frame cracked and popped apart a few inches at the seams.

Raven gasped. It was working! The queen was destroying the mirror!

The king stepped back. "Melantha! Yes!"

Green smoke began to pour from the mirror again, but this time it faded as soon as it touched the ground. With a loud groaning shout, she pushed again and then said, "Mirror, I command you to destroy yourself! Let. Me. Go! My husband's love is ten times more powerful than you are!" She strained again and this time the glass of the mirror cracked. A small line fissured from her neck up to the frame. With another groan, the mirror gave in a great explosion of shattered glass.

Raven and Terrance ducked as shards flew at them and then dissolved before their eyes. When Raven looked up, she beheld her mother—the mother she had always known, in her fair skinned, red-haired glory, standing in front of them all. She wore her gold wedding gown and had never looked more enchanting.

"Melantha?" Herbert asked as he stepped toward her.

"Yes." She glanced around the room as if seeing everyone for the first time. "It is me. I am back."

He stepped forward and wrapped his arms around her. "I love you!"

Almost in a daze, she slowly folded her arms around him and then whispered, "I love you more."

When she pulled away, there were tears glistening in her eyes. "Thank you." And then she searched the crowd. "Snow?"

Corlan held her. "Yes?" she said, but did not step forward.

"I do not expect forgiveness for anything I have done, but know that I vow never to wish you harm again."

"Corlan?" She nodded at him and then said, "Raven?" She searched until she found her. "I am sorry for what I have done to you as well. I promise I will do everything in my power to make it up to you both."

"Perhaps," King Herbert said with a shaky breath as he grinned, "it is better you do not try to do things in your power. Mayhap it is best if you do things as well as you can and allow the rest to sort itself out."

Melantha looked at him seriously for a moment and then rested her head upon his shoulder. "I think I shall take each day one step at a time, and relearn what truly makes me happy."

"I love you," he said to her.

Suddenly Melantha slipped to her knees and began to weep. "What have I become? I do not deserve any of this, and yet, you are too kind. You are too good. How will I ever rise above that monster I turned into?"

"It was not you, Mother," Raven said. "It never was. We always knew it was the mirror behind it all."

King Herbert knelt down. Placing his arm around her, he said, "Every day will prove itself brighter—every single day. Now that you are out of the mirror's clutches, you shall truly begin to heal. No matter what tomorrow brings, know that I will always love you. And if I have breath in my body, I will use it to prove that."

***

AND HE DID. KING Herbert and Queen Melantha ruled in peace for the rest of their years together. Their kingdom was one of graciousness and love. And thankfully, due to the harsh lessons of the mirror, Melantha learned to settle into helping those nearest to her and allowing them the peace they deserved. No longer did she desire for the power to save the world—only the ability to help those closest.

Corlan and Snow soon wed in the spring with tulips in full bloom all around them. And he moved her to his castle in the kingdom next door—the castle he grew up in. They ended up having seven children, three stalwart princes whom they named Truth, Brave, and Peace, and four princesses who bore the names of Grace, Hope, Joy, and Love. They ruled their kingdom using those seven gifts all seven days of the week and truly found eternal happiness.

It took a bit more convincing for Terrance and Raven to see how they perfectly belonged to one another. However, at the wedding feast for Corlan and Snow, Terrance bowed low and presented Raven with a golden ring engraved with the words "Forever yours, forever true." He did so with such flourish and with those dashed dimples peeking out, she could do nothing but weep and accept the love he offered, for even she knew it was time.

After the wedding, they moved to the Sybright court, where she happily ruled with him for the longest of the three couples. They had two strapping sons and a delightful daughter who was just as quick-witted as her parents but had all the charm of her father. At least that is what her mother would say each time she looked at her daughter's divine dimples.

And so we see in this tale the beginnings of three different stories, all wrapped around one eternal purpose—to love with all thy heart. For this is the story of kings and queens who overcame their fears, learned to battle the worst within them, and grew in patience to mature into who they were destined to become.

And each and every one of them lived happily ever after.

The End

Also in the Jenni James Faerie Tale Collection:

The Frog Prince

CHAPTER ONE

HIS ROYAL HIGHNESS PRINCE Nolan turned to his mother, Queen Bethany of Hollene Court, and announced, "I have decided to do it!" He threw the missive from his intended, Princess Blythe McKenna, upon the small end table near the settee in the formal drawing room where his mother preferred to take her tea.

"You decided to do what, dear?" his mother asked as she sipped at her cup.

"I have decided to visit Blythe in disguise." He sighed and sat down across from her in a green-and-white striped overstuffed chair. "I must meet her in person. I can't ascertain from her letters what she is truly like. It is a great muddle, and it is time I decided once and for all if I will indeed offer my hand or not."

"But you are already promised to each other!" She set her cup upon the saucer and placed them both on the end table. "What is this nonsense?"

"Mother, it is not nonsense. Betrothing me as an infant is not something I can accept, especially when I am quite unsure whether my bride-to-be is a spoiled child or a blessed saint."

She gasped. "Nolan! Watch your tongue." She never did enjoy his mention of saints as general cant.

Nolan sighed. "Forgive me. But there is something so self-possessed about her letters that quite causes me to scowl. I have got to sort this out for myself before any royal announcements are made. It is time I approached this differently, visited her as an uninvited guest, and saw how she would treat me."

"My goodness!" The queen's hand flew to her prominent bosom, the plum ruffles of her gown doing much to make her appear rounder and plumper than she actually was. "What do you plan to do, Nolan? Disguise yourself as a pauper or some such?" She looked truly scandalized.

He chuckled to himself. Perhaps it was the mischief-maker in him, or perhaps he enjoyed unsettling her feathers, but whatever the reason, he took pleasure in watching his mother's reactions. At times they were simply invaluable. "No, not a pauper. I have decided to take it a step further than that."

"How shall you disguise yourself, then?"

"Perhaps … as an animal?"

"I beg your pardon?" Her arms swung out, one violently upsetting the tea things upon the end table so they came crashing down upon the floor and shattering. One fragment skittered across the marble flooring to nudge his shiny boot. Normally his mother would be aghast at the mess and insist it be cleaned immediately. However, this time it was as if she did not know it had happened. "Why in all the great heavens would you decide to take on the form of some animal? You, Prince Nolan! One of the handsomest men who has ever walked the halls of this great court—you now wish to present yourself to your betrothed as an … an …" Her voice trickled off as she began to sway.

"Mother, do not swoon. It does not become you," he said languidly as he slowly leaned forward, ready to assist if need be.

Bethany sat up. "I do not swoon! I have never swooned."

"Just so."

"But why must you appear as an animal? What will they think of us? Nolan, this can't be right. You must consider a less ludicrous scheme."

He laughed. "No. It is perfect—how else will I be able to learn what this girl is really like? If I come to her dashing and princely, she will no doubt be quite smitten, as they all are. But if I come to her as, say, a dog or something, she is bound to show her true character."

"A dog! My son, a *dog*. I can't bear it. I can't even think such a thing. It is not the right animal at all!"

"Perhaps you are correct." He thought about it for a few moments. "A dog might be a little too easy. Far too many people love dogs."

"Well, it is good to know you are finally speaking some sense!"

"No, I must plan on something much more hideous."

"More hideous? Nolan!"

He folded his arms. "Yes, something all girls detest and run screaming from."

"You would not dare! This is all some hoax, is it not? You are merely jesting your mother, like you and Sariah did when you were children, constantly pulling those maddening pranks upon me. Tell me this is one of your larks. Tell me."

"I am afraid not, Mother." He stood and walked toward her.

"Then why? I do not understand," she said. "What are your plans? Will you simply put on a costume, or—"

He leaned down and kissed her cheek. "No. I will not wear a costume. I plan to ask the village herb woman to put a charm over me."

"Nolan!"

"Not for long, perhaps thirty days or so. But I need to know for myself if she is indeed the woman of my dreams, or if my instincts are correct and she will prove to be more of a handful than I am willing to take on."

"But you can't back out of your betrothal now!" the queen exclaimed.

"I can't back out of anything that I was not asked to be a part of. The design was yours and Queen Mary Elizabeth's, not mine." When she gasped once more, he quickly added, "I promise not to break anything off hastily. I will wait the full thirty days before doing so."

"Nolan, you are out of your wits!"

"No, Mother, I feel for the first time in my life that I am finally doing something especially intelligent. If Princess Blythe can prove me wrong and is indeed the woman I desire, she will want for nothing in all the land. I intend to treat my wife with the utmost of courtesy and devote all my life to creating a magical existence with her. However, she must pass this small test first, because as spoiled as she seems to be, it is better to know that I would indeed be marrying a princess and not a harpy!"

"Nolan, I will never ever understand you as long as I live."

"Good." He grinned. "Then my work here is done."

His mother paused before saying, "Do you mean to tell me that you shall turn yourself into an animal for thirty days?"

"Yes, precisely."

"And you will look just like this animal."

"Yes."

"And poor Blythe McKenna has thirty days to treat you kindly, and then once she does, you will turn back into a prince and offer your hand to her?"

"Hmm … I do see some flaws there." He sat back down upon the striped chair. "Perhaps if she does something sooner that would prove her kind heart—perhaps I would have the charm bring me back to my princely form earlier."

Bethany shook her head as if he were completely foolish. "What would you have her do?"

All at once Nolan smiled. "I have it! Princess Blythe must kiss me!"

"Kiss an animal?" She fluttered her hand. "You are mad!"

"Oh, I hope so. This will only be entertaining if I do have some touch of madness in me." He winked.

"My word." She sighed. "What animal have you decided to become?"

"The most revolting, un-kiss-worthy creature I can think of."

"And that is?"

"A frog." He chuckled at her appalled face. "Yes, I shall be a frog prince."

ABOUT JENNI

Jenni James is the busy mom of eleven children (seven hers, three her hubby's, and one theirs). She's also the mom of fifty book babies and sixteen screenplays too. When she isn't dreaming of creating new stories, she's chasing her kids around the house. She lives in a cottage nestled in the tops of the Utah mountains with peacocks, chickens, ducks, geese, turkeys and her beautiful keeshond named Holly.

Jenni loves to hear from her readers. You can email her at
thejennijames@gmail.com
Or snail mail at:
Jenni James
PO Box 449
Fountain Green, UT 84632